D1644960

I
T

re
ke
a

req
given

A
cove

B
Dry, an
book ha
disease
Departn

RETURN

20SEI

28 DE

14 FEB

21 APR

23 JUL

E-1

24 S

-3 NOV 1

21 JAN 1957

a30118 027934136b

A CHARACTER IN DISTRESS

A Character in Distress

by
Luigi Pirandello

13703
N. PIR

Duckworth
3 Henrietta Street, London, W.C. 2

First published 1938
All rights reserved

02793413

RAWTENSTALL
5 - AUG. 1941
PUBLIC LIBRARY

PRINTED IN GREAT BRITAIN
BY WESTERN PRINTING SERVICES LTD., BRISTOL

SB

CONTENTS

PLEASE DO NOT SOIL, MARK, OR
OTHERWISE INJURE THIS BOOK.

A CHARACTER IN DISTRESS

It has for a long time been my habit to receive in audience, every Sunday morning, the characters of my future stories.

Five hours it lasts, from eight to one.

Almost invariably I find myself in bad company.

I don't know why, but as a rule these audiences of mine seem to be attended by the most disgruntled people in the world, with whom it is a terrible strain to have to deal; either they are afflicted with some strange malady, or else involved in the most extraordinary circumstances.

Patiently I listen to all of them and question them politely. I make a note of their names and take particulars of each of them; I keep a record of their feelings and aspirations. I must, however, add that, unfortunately for me, I am not easily satisfied. I can bear a lot, quite politely, too, but I don't like being fooled. Also, I always want to penetrate to the depths of their souls by long and exhaustive research.

7

Now, it has happened that more than one amongst them have taken exception to my questions, becoming sulky and obstreperously stubborn, perhaps because they thought I revel in robbing them of that earnestness which they invariably assume when they first introduce themselves to me.

Patiently, gently I endeavour to make them see and realize that my questions are not superfluous. It is easy to want to be this or that, but it remains to be seen whether we have the power to change into what we would like to be. If such power be lacking, then our pretensions cannot appear otherwise than ridiculous and futile.

Unfortunately, my characters refuse to recognize this. And then I pity them, for I am good-natured at heart. At the same time certain misfortunes cannot be pitied without provoking laughter.

Anyway, the characters of my stories go about the world, denouncing me as a cruel and heartless writer. What is needed is a sympathetic critic who would show how much there is of compassion behind that laughter.

But where are the sympathetic critics of to-day?

.　　.　　.　　.　　.

A CHARACTER IN DISTRESS

I must point out that at these interviews certain characters push their way in front of all
others and assert themselves with such cheek and
impudence that I am forced, at times, to dismiss
them without delay. Later, many of them bitterly
repent their display of temper and implore me
to put right one or other of their faults in their
make-up. Then I smile and tell them they must
make amends for their original sin and wait until
I have time and opportunity to return to them.

Amongst those who stand waiting at the back
of the overcrowded room, some show signs of
distress, some get cross and some get tired and go
and knock at the door of some other author.

It happens quite frequently that I find in the
works of many of my colleagues certain characters who had previously presented themselves to
me; on the other hand, it has happened that I
have spotted some who, not satisfied with the
way I had dealt with them, refused to try and give
a better account of themselves elsewhere.

I don't mind because as a rule two or three
new ones present themselves to me every week.
Often the crowd is such that I have to listen to
more than one of them at the same time. But
there comes a moment when my brain, divided

and confused, revolts at this double and **triple** occupation, becomes exasperated and demands that they should talk one at a time, softly and quietly, or else go to hell.

I shall always remember the infinite resignation with which a poor old man, who had come a long distance to see me, awaited his turn. He was a teacher named Icilio Saporini. At the fall of the Roman Republic in 1849 he had been banished to America for composing a patriotic song. After forty-five years, when nearly eighty years old, he had come back to Italy to die. Exceedingly polite, his thin voice reminiscent of the buzz of a mosquito, he allowed everyone else to pass in front of him. At last, one day when I was still convalescent after a long illness, I saw him enter my room, all self-deprecation, with a timid smile on his lips.

"May I? . . . If you don't mind. . . ."

"Yes, do come in, my dear little old man." He had chosen the most suitable moment, and I made him die at once in a short story, called "Old Music."

.   .   .   .   .

This last Sunday I entered my study a little

later than usual for the audience. A long novel, which somebody had given me, and which had been waiting for me more than a month to be read, kept me awake until three a.m. by the many thoughts aroused in me by one of the characters in the book—the only live one amongst so many colourless shadows.

It described a poor old man, a certain Doctor Fileno, who thought he had found an efficacious remedy for all human ills, an infallible recipe capable of bringing solace to himself and all mankind in case of any calamity whatever, public or private.

Actually it was more than a remedy or a recipe that Doctor Fileno had discovered; it was a method consisting in reading history books from morning till night and practising looking at the present as though it were an event already buried in the archives of the past. By this method he had cured himself of all suffering and of all worry, and without having to die had found a stern, serene peace, imbued with that peculiar sadness which cemeteries would still preserve even if all men on earth were dead.

But Doctor Fileno had never even dreamt of drawing on the past standards for the present.

He knew that it would have been waste of time, and stupid waste at that, for history is an idealized composition of elements selected by the historians according to their personal feelings, sympathies, antipathies, aspirations and opinions, preventing one from making use of this idealized composition, which keeps on moving, while its elements remain scattered and unruly. Nor did he ever dream of drawing on the present rules and forecasts for the future. Indeed, he was doing exactly the opposite. He was trying to project himself into an imaginary future in order to look at the present, and he succeeded in viewing it as if it were the past.

For instance, he had lost a daughter a few days before. A friend called to condole with him in his grief, but he found him already consoled as if that child had been dead for more than a hundred years. Although his grief was still recent, very recent, he had succeeded in relegating it to the past, pushing it back into time. This, however, did not prevent him from talking of his tragedy from the loftiest viewpoint and with a great sense of dignity.

Briefly, Doctor Fileno had invented a kind of inverted telescope for himself. He opened it out, not to look at the future, where he knew there would be nothing to see, but he tried to convince himself that by looking through it from the larger end through the smaller lens and by directing it to the present, all events would immediately become diminutive and distant. At the same time he was working at a book, *The Philosophy of Distance*, which would undoubtedly have created a sensation.

While I was reading the novel, it became apparent to me that the author—completely absorbed in holding together one of the tritest stories—had found himself unable to understand this character, who in himself contained the germ of a real creation. But for a time the character had succeeded in escaping from the author, in cutting himself loose and superimposing himself vigorously upon the banal story of the book. Then all of a sudden, deformed and enfeebled, he had allowed himself to be bent to the exigencies of a wrong and silly ending.

My imagination aroused, I remained there for a long time in the stillness of the night, with the picture of this character before me. What a pity! There was enough material there to build a masterpiece, provided always that the author had not so miserably misunderstood his character and neglected him, and had made him the central figure of the story. All those artificialities which he had introduced might perhaps have transformed themselves, might have become alive too. A great sorrow and considerable resentment got hold of me because of that life which had remained so miserably unfulfilled.

. . . . .

On entering my study late on that particular morning, I found unusual confusion there, for that Doctor Fileno had already forced his way amongst my other waiting characters, who got angry and nasty and went for him, trying to push him back, to throw him out.

"Now then," I said. "Ladies and gentlemen, what is all this about? And you, Doctor Fileno, what do you want here? I have already wasted too much time on you. You don't belong to me. Leave me alone to look after my own characters. Go away!"

So deep and desperate a sorrow marred the face of Doctor Fileno that all the other characters felt sorry for him and retired.

"Do not send me away, please, do not send me away! Grant me but five minutes if these ladies and gentlemen will permit, and let me explain, please!"

Perplexed, but moved to compassion, I asked him:

"Explain what? I am perfectly sure, dear doctor, that you deserved to have fallen into better hands, but what can I do for you now? I have already expressed my regrets, and that is all I can do."

"All you can do? By God, no!" burst out Doctor Fileno, while his whole body seemed to shake with indignation. "You say that, because I do not belong to you. Believe me, your neglect, your scorn would be less cruel than this passive pity, which, I am sorry to say, is unworthy of an artist. Nobody understands characters better than you; nobody knows better than you do that we are live beings, more alive than those of flesh and blood; perhaps less real, but more true. One comes into the world in various ways, dear sir, and you are well aware that nature uses the human imagination to carry on her creative work. Whosoever is born through this creative activity which resides in the spirit of man is ordained by nature to a life far superior to those who are born from the womb of woman. He who is born

a character, who has the great gift of being born
a live character, can even scorn death. He will
never die. Man will die, the author will die—he
is only the natural instrument of his creation—
but the character remains immortal. To remain
immortal does not require extraordinary gifts nor
the accomplishment of miraculous deeds. Tell
me, who was Sancho Panza? Tell me, who was
Don Abbondio? Yet they have eternal life, because they are vital germs who had the luck of
finding a fertile womb, a brain that knew how
to raise and nurse them."

"Yes, dear doctor," I said. "This is all very
well, but I still fail to see what you want from
me."

"Oh, you fail to see? Have I perhaps come to
the wrong place? Or am I loafing about the
moon? What sort of a writer are you then?
Dare you really say that you do not understand
the horror of my tragedy? To have the in-
estimable privilege of being born a character—
and in our times—I mean in times so beset with
demeaning difficulties, which hinder, deform and
enfeeble human existence. To have the privilege
of being born a live character, to have been
ordained—even in my small way—to immortality

and yet, just through bad luck, to have fallen into those hands, to be condemned to an iniquitous death, to be forced to live in that artificial world where I can neither breathe nor move because everything is faked, false, prearranged, protracted? Mere words and paper! Paper and words! A human being who finds himself involved in such conditions, and who cannot or will not subject himself to them, can free himself of them, and run away, but a poor character cannot—he must remain nailed to eternal martyrdom. Air, air, life!

"Just look at me ... Fileno! ... he has called me Fileno! ... Do you really think my name should be Fileno? Idiot, idiot! Not even a name was he able to give me. Fileno! And why should he come to me, the author of *The Philosophy of Distance*, to make me end in such a miserable way and make me solve all that stupid muddle of his plot? Instead of Negroni, the solicitor, he had to force me to marry as her second husband that fool Graziella. Don't try to make excuses for him. These, my dear sir, are crimes which should be avenged with blood and tears. But what will happen now instead? Nothing. Silence. Or perhaps a few slating lines in two or three papers.

Perhaps a critic will write: 'A pity about that poor Doctor Fileno! He was really a good character!' And there the whole thing will end. Condemned to death, that is what I am, I, the author of *The Philosophy of Distance*, which that idiot who is my author was not even able to get published at my expense. Terrible, sir, terrible! Don't let us think about it any more. To work, and quickly, dear sir. Rescue me at once, at once. Make me live, you who understand all the life that is in me."

At the conclusion of this passionate outburst, I could only answer with a long look at Doctor Fileno's face.

"You think it might upset my author?" he resumed anxiously. "You think it might upset him. But isn't it a legitimate proposal? Haven't you the undeniable right to make me your own and give me the life which that idiot has not been able to give me? It is your right, it is mine too—you do understand, don't you?"

"It may be your right, dear doctor," I answered. "It may be even a legitimate right, as you seem to believe. But I never do such things. It is useless for you to plead. I simply will not do it. Try someone else."

"And to whom can I apply if you . . ."

"I don't know. Perhaps you will find some-body who is perfectly convinced of the legitimacy of this right. Just a minute, dear Doctor Fileno, I have an idea. Are you or are you not the author of *The Philosophy of Distance*?"

"How could I not be?" the doctor burst out, jumping to his feet and placing his hand on his heart, as a sign that he was speaking the truth. "Of course I am. How dare you doubt it? Oh, I understand. It is always because of that mur-derer of mine. Unable to realize all that was to be got out of my discovery of the inverted tele-scope, he merely gave a brief résumé of my theories. . . ."

I put out my hand as he was getting too near me. Then I smiled and said:

"All right, all right! But why do you. . . ."

"Why do I? . . ."

"Yes, why do you grumble at your author? Have you yourself been able to take advantage of your theory? This is precisely what I want to tell you. Let me explain. If you really believe in the virtue of your philosophy, even as I do, why do you not apply it to your own case. You are trying to find—and in our times—a writer amongst us who will give you immortality. But just read what all the most important critics say of us poor little contemporary writers. We are, and yet we are not, my dear doctor. Why not submit—as we are doing—the most important events, the most burning questions and the most marvellous modern works to the famous inverted telescope? My dear doctor, I think if you will do this you will not see anyone or anything any more. Therefore try to console yourself, or if you prefer, be satisfied with your lot; and let me now hold audience with my own poor characters, who may be bad, but are less extravagant in their ambitions."

THE BEAUTY AND THE BEAST

THERE can be no doubt that Mr. Charles Trockley
is right. In fact, I am even willing to admit that
Mr. Charles Trockley could never be wrong,
because right and Mr. Trockley are one and the
same thing. Mr. Charles Trockley's every movement, every look and every word are so definite,
so precise, and so exact that anyone must surely
see how impossible it would be for Mr. Trockley
to be wrong in any circumstances, in any incident
which may happen to him, or in the answer of
any question that may be put to him.

For instance, he and I were born in the same
year, the same month, and almost the same
day. He was born in England, I in Sicily. To-day
—June 15th—he celebrates his forty-eighth
birthday. I, too, shall celebrate my forty-eighth
year on the 28th of this month. Very well, how
old then shall we be next year, he on the 15th and
I on the 28th of June? Mr. Trockley is not
flummoxed for a moment, does not hesitate for a

minute; with complete confidence he asserts that on the 15th and the 28th of June next year, he and I respectively will be a year older and that, therefore, we shall be forty-nine.

Well who could say that Mr. Charles Trockley is wrong?

.   .   .   .   .

Time does not deal alike with all of us. I might in one day, in one hour, get more damaged than he could be in the course of ten years, considering his general well-being and strict self-discipline. On the other hand, in view of the deplorable unruliness of my spirit, I might in one year live more than an entire life. My body, weaker and much less cared for than his, has endured far more wear and tear in these past forty-eight years, than Mr. Trockley's is likely to sustain in seventy years. This is substantiated by the fact that although his hair is silver-white, his boiled lobster face does not as yet show a single wrinkle, and every morning he can do his fencing exercises with juvenile agility.

Well, what about it? Any such consideration of brain and fact are, for Mr. Charles Trockley, absolutely meaningless, remote from reason.

THE BEAUTY AND THE BEAST

Reason tells Mr. Charles Trockley that, according to arithmetic, he and I, on June 15th and 28th of next year, will be one year older and, therefore, forty-nine years old.

After this statement, listen to what recently happened to Mr. Charles Trockley, and try, if you can, to say that he was wrong.

. . . . .

Last April, following the usual itinerary laid down by Baedecker for a journey to Italy, Miss Ethel Holloway, the charming and vivacious daughter of Sir W. H. Holloway, one of the wealthiest and most influential members of the House of Commons, arrived in Girgenti, Sicily, to visit the marvellous ruins of the ancient Doric city. Charmed by the entrancing sea coast which, during that month, is all covered with white almond blossoms, and by the warm breezes of the African sea, she decided to stay a day longer at the Hotel des Temples, which is situated just outside the rocky and poor townlet of to-day, right in the open country, in a most delightful spot.

For twenty-two years Mr. Charles Trockley had been Vice-Consul for England at Girgenti, and every day, at sunset, for twenty-two years he had walked, with his elastic and well-measured gait, from the upper town on the hill to the ruins of the lofty and majestic Acragantine Temples, on that rocky boundary which puts a stop to the slope of a neighbouring hill, the Acrean hill, upon which once stood, resplendent with marbles, the ancient town exalted by Pindar as the most beautiful amongst all mortal cities.

According to the Ancients, the Agracantians used to eat every day as if they were doomed to die on the following day, and built their houses as if they had been destined never to die. But little do they eat to-day, because great is the poverty in the town and country, and after so many wars, seven fires and as many sackings, no trace is left of the houses of the ancient town.

On their site there is a grove of almond and sarracin olive-trees, which is therefore called the Grove of the City. The hairy, ashen olive-trees reach in a long tongue towards the columns of the majestic temples, seemingly praying for those abandoned slopes. Beneath the crest runs—when there is any water—the river Acragas, which Pindar sang for its magnificent flux.

Small flocks of goat still climb the stony river-bed, climb up the stony bridge and stretch themselves out or chew the meagre grass in the solemn shadows of the ancient Concord Temple, which is still intact. The goatherd, coarse and sleepy as an Arab, also stretches himself out on the dilapidated steps of the forecourt to the temple, drawing a few doleful notes from his can flute.

To Mr. Charles Trockley this intrusion of the goats into the precincts of the temple always seemed a horrible profanation and on innumerable occasions he had lodged formal complaints with the custodians of the monument, without, however, obtaining any other answer than a philosophical smile of resignation, or a shrug of the shoulder. With genuine shudders of indignation, Mr. Charles Trockley told me of those smiles and shoulder shrugs on occasions when I accompanied him on his walks.

It often happened that in the Temple of Concord, or in the higher one, that of Hera Licinia, or in the one commonly called the Temple of Giants, Mr. Trockley would meet some of his countrymen who had come to visit the ruins. To all and sundry of them he remarked—with that indignation which neither time nor habit had minimized—on the profanation of those resting or chewing goats in the shadows of the temple columns.

But to tell the truth, not all the English tourists shared Mr. Trockley's indignation. Indeed, for some of them the sight of those dozing goats in the temples which had been left solitary and abandoned in a forgotten country, held a measure of poetry. More than one—to the extreme outrage of Mr. Trockley—even admired the sight and declared himself delighted with it.

None, however, were more pleased and delighted with the sight than the young and vivacious Miss Ethel Holloway last April. In fact, while the indignant vice-consul was imparting to her some invaluable archæological information never yet mentioned in Baedecker or any other guide, she was rude enough to turn her back on him and run after a delightful black kid, which had only been born a few days previously, and which was scampering right and left amongst the outstretched goats, as if lured by hundreds of luminous mosquitoes in the air, then suddenly looking scared at its own daring and perilous scampers, for even the slightest noise, the slightest breath of air, the slightest shadow in this uncertain business of life, still caused it to tremble from head to tail from sheer timidity.

On that day I happened to be with Mr. Trockley, and although I was delighted to see the young girl who had so suddenly fallen in love with the little black goat and wanted to buy it at any price, yet I was also sorry for what Mr. Trockley had to suffer in consequence.

"Buy this kid?"

"Yes, yes. Buy it at once."

She too was trembling, little Miss Ethel, just like that dear little black animal, perhaps never even suspecting that she could not have done a worse turn to Mr. Trockley, who had hated these animals ferociously for a long time.

In vain did Mr. Trockley try to dissuade her, to explain to her all the troubles that would arise from such a purchase. At last he had to give in, and, if only as a sign of respect to her father, he approached the objectionable goatherd and bargained for the purchase of the black kid.

Miss Ethel Holloway, having paid the money for the purchase, told Mr. Trockley that she would entrust her pet to the manager of the Hotel des Temples, and that, as soon as she was back in London, she would wire for the dear little thing to be sent to her, all expenses paid, and she drove back to her hotel, carrying in her arms the bleating and struggling young goat.

Outlined against the sun which was setting in a mirage-like fretwork of clouds, swimming above the sea which looked like a vast golden mirror, I saw that fair-haired girl, slim and radiant, fade out in a black carriage, immersed in a shimmering cloud of light; it looked almost like a dream.

Suddenly I realized that to have been able, so far from her own country, and so completely detached from her own surroundings and attachments, to conceive such a great desire and affection for a diminutive black kid, the girl could not have possessed a crumb of that stodgy reasoning power, that stolidity, which governed every thought, step and word of Mr. Charles Trockley.

But what did little Miss Ethel Holloway have in place of that reasoning power?

"Nothing but stupidity," is Mr. Charles Trockley's retort, uttered with a fierceness painful to see in a man usually so reserved.

The reason of this fury is due to the events which followed the purchase of that black kid.

.   .   .   .   .

Miss Ethel Holloway left Girgenti the following day. From Sicily she went to Greece, from Greece to Egypt and from Egypt to India.

She arrived back in London almost eight months later, and considering the adventures she must have experienced on her long journey it would be nothing short of a miracle if Miss Holloway remembered the black kid she had bought on that far distant day amongst the ruins of the Acragantine Temples of Sicily. Nevertheless and as agreed, as soon as she arrived back she wrote to Mr. Charles Trockley and claimed her pet.

Now, every year, the Hotel des Temples shuts down in the middle of June and does not open again till early November. The manager to whom Miss Holloway had entrusted her pet kid had in his turn handed it over to the caretaker of the hotel, but without any special recommendation; on the contrary, he seemed to be rather irritated at the trouble the little animal had given and was still giving him.

From day to day the caretaker waited for Mr. Trockley, who, as the manager had told him, would come to fetch the young goat and ship it to England. Eventually, as no one came, he thought it best to return the young goat to the goatherd from whom Miss Holloway had bought it, assuring him that he would have kept it for ever were there not the chance of the young girl claiming it again, and promising that in the event of the vice-consul claiming it, he would refund him for his troubles and pasturage.

When, about eight months later, Miss Holloway's letter arrived from London, the manager of the Hotel des Temples, the caretaker and the goatherd, all found themselves in a terrible mess; the manager for having entrusted the kid to the caretaker, the caretaker for having passed it on to the goatherd, and the latter for having handed it on to another goatherd, together with the promises that had been made to him.

The search went on for over a month, but it seemed impossible to find any trace of this second goatherd.

Then one fine day, at the British Vice-Consulate of Girgenti, Mr. Trockley found himself presented with a horrible, horned, evil-smelling, nasty beast, its bloated skin a reddish colour, encrusted with excrements and mud; with menacingly bent head it snorted deep and loud, apparently demanding to know what was required of it in such an unaccustomed place.

As was usual with him, Mr. Trockley did not betray the slightest symptoms of fright; not one tremor of agitation passed through him. He just jotted up the time which had elapsed since the first day of April and the last days of December and came to the conclusion that by all that was reasonable the charming little black kid of yore might easily have grown into this huge, dirty beast of to-day. Without a moment's hesitation he wrote to Miss Holloway that he would have it shipped from Porto Empedocle by the first homeward-bound British ship.

Round the neck of this loathsome beast he tied a small label on which Miss Holloway's address was written, and gave orders for the animal to be taken to the docks. There, endangering his personal dignity, and followed by a crowd of urchins, he himself led the struggling animal by a long rope to the boat which was to carry it to England. Having handed it over, he returned to Girgenti, completely satisfied of having scrupulously fulfilled a contract, which he had undertaken not so much because of Miss Ethel Holloway's deplorable stupidity, but because of the consideration due to her father.

· · · · ·

Yesterday Mr Charles Trockley came to see me at my home. He was in such a state of physical and moral collapse that I ran at once to his assistance, asked him to sit down and fetched him a glass of water.

"For heaven's sake, Mr. Trockley, what has happened to you?"

Unable to speak, Mr. Trockley took a letter from his pocket and handed it to me.

It was from Sir W. H. Holloway, member of the House of Commons, and it was covered with invectives, accusing Mr. Trockley of insulting his daughter, Miss Ethel, by sending her that loathsome filthy beast.

And such were the thanks Mr. Trockley got for shouldering all those troubles.

But what was that silly Miss Holloway expecting? Did she think that after eleven months there would be delivered to her in London, the same black kid that was scampering about, tiny and all shining, trembling with timidity amongst the columns of the ancient Greek Temple of Sicily. Could such a thing be possible? Mr. Trockley could not yet console himself.

Seeing him before me in such a state, I tried to comfort him as best I could, agreeing that a creature like Miss Holloway must be absolutely devoid of common sense as well as capricious.

"Stupid! Stupid!! Stupid!!!"

"It would be better to call her unreasonable, my dear Mr. Trockley, my friend. But you see" (I ventured to add very timidly) "she left here last April. In her mind's eye she took with her the image of that dear little black kid. Now let us be fair; however unreasonable it may seem to you. You could not reasonably expect her to welcome that full-grown goat which you presented to her with such sudden reality."

"But then," asked Mr. Trockley, standing up and measuring himself with me, though there was no malice in his eyes, "what should I have done according to your views?"

Thoroughly embarrassed, I hastened to say:

"I would not like to appear to you as unreasonable as your young countrywoman from across the water, but had I been in your place, Mr. Trockley, do you know what I would have done? Either I would have written to Miss Holloway saying that her dear little pet was dead for want of her kisses and caresses, or else I would have bought another little kid, just as tiny and shiny, the perfect facsimile of the one she had bought last April, and I would have sent it to her, feeling quite sure that Miss Ethel Holloway would not have dreamed that her baby goat could not have remained for eleven months just as she had left it. By this, my dear Mr. Trockley, my friend, you will perceive that I think Miss Ethel Holloway was completely unreasonable and that reason is entirely on your side, as always."

THE HAUNTED HOUSE

Mᴉᴄᴇ are never aware of the trap when they fall into one. Would they ever be caught if they knew that one had been laid for them? And even when they have been caught, they seem unable to realize where they are, and keep scuttling madly right and left, poking their whiskered little noses through the bars, squeaking and squealing in desperate endeavour to find a way out.

On the other hand, when a man starts litigation, he knows perfectly well that he is walking into a trap. But while the mouse struggles the man stays quiet—quiet of course with his body; inside—that is mentally—he behaves exactly like the mouse, if not worse.

This was, in fact, what was happening to the crowd of clients who, covered with perspiration and eaten alive by the flies and the boredom, were sitting on that sweltering August morning in the waiting-room of the Lawyer Zummo, awaiting their turn to consult him.

None of them moved from their seats but the glances of wild hatred exchanged between them could leave no doubt as to their thoughts. Each would have liked the lawyer exclusively to himself, and each felt that, with so many clients to interview in the same morning, there would be little time available for them all. Besides, with that big crowd to handle, with that frightful heat of ninety degrees in the shade, with so many different points to argue, would the lawyer's mind still be as clear as the case required?

Every time that the clerk, who was sitting at a desk copying notes at a frantic speed, glanced at the clock, two or three clients would sigh for boredom, while others, exhausted from the heat and the long wait, would keep their eyes glued on the big, dusty bookcases overloaded with legal papers—the scourge and ruin of so many unhappy families. Others still, trying to look indifferent, would peer through the green shutters of the window into the street where people were walking happy and careless whilst they. . . . Phew!—and with a furious gesture of the hand they would flick off the flies made wilder and more aggressive than ever through the heat and the heavy perspiration.

36

Even more troublesome than the flies was the lawyer's little son, a brat of ten, barefooted and unkempt, who had obviously run away from the adjoining house to cheer up papa's clients.

"What's your name?" "What's that locket?" "How does it open?" "What's inside?" "A lock of hair?" "Whose hair is it?" "Why do you keep it?"

Then, hearing papa nearing the door to escort some important client, he would suddenly dive beneath the table, and hide himself between the legs of the clerk.

Everyone in the waiting-room would rise to his feet, each client looking beseechingly at the lawyer, who would raise both hands, saying: "Patience, my friends, one at a time."

The lucky one would follow him obsequiously, shutting the door behind him while the others would sit down again to their exasperating and oppressive wait.

.   .   .   .   .

Three clients only, who seemed to be husband, wife and daughter, showed no sign of impatience. The husband—a man in his sixties—had a gloomy, almost mournful appearance. He had obstinately refused to remove a ruffled, greenish, wide-brimmed top-hat which no doubt he considered the most appropriate accessory to the heavy, old-fashioned frock-coat stinking of naphthaline. It was quite obvious that this dress had been chosen out of deference for the occasion, an official interview with a lawyer.

Yet he was not perspiring.

Pale to the extreme, he looked almost bloodless, his jaw and cheeks being thinly covered with a layer of mouldy greyish fur. His light grey eyes, set close to a massive nose, had a squint, and, bent on his chair, with his head drooping and his thin hands resting on a stick, he looked almost crushed by some intolerable load. At his side, with a defiant look of flashing stupidity sat his wife.

Stout and thriving, with a pronounced bust, she seemed unable to unglue from the ceiling a pair of beautiful jet black eyes staring from her somewhat whiskered red face.

Next to her sat their daughter—thin, pale and squinting like her father—almost a cripple. It nearly looked—watching them together—as if only the presence of the stout woman between father and daughter could prevent them from falling to the ground.

The three had aroused the intense curiosity of the other clients, for three times the poor things had allowed newcomers to take their turn, alleging that their case was so important that it would require a very long interview with the lawyer.

What could have happened to them? Who was threatening them? Perhaps a vendetta or a murder? Perhaps financial ruin?

No, it could not be financial ruin. The wife was loaded with gold; large ear-rings dangled from her ears; a double chain was choking her neck: a large golden locket was going up and down on her bosom: a long gold chain was securing her fan and valuable rings covered her stumpy fingers. What then had brought them there to consult the lawyer Zummo?

Little by little all the clients were being received by the lawyer but the three would remain sitting there—motionless and disinterested—deeply absorbed in their own thoughts. Only every now and then the wife would make use of her fan or the man would lean forward to the child to remind her:

"Tinina . . . remember the thimble."

Some of the clients tried hard to push the

lawyer's brat towards the three, but even the child—scared by those mournful faces—would have nothing to do with them.

And when—it was about noon—all the clients had gone, the three were still sitting there, motionless and dumb like statues, glued to their chairs:

"Well, have you fallen asleep? Why are you waiting to go in?" shouted the clerk, raising his head and getting impatient.

"May we?" asked the man apologetically while the three rose to their feet.

"Of course you may; you should have gone in before," reproached the clerk. "Don't you know that it's nearly lunch time? And, by the way, what's your name?"

The man at last removed his top-hat, uncovering at the same time the torture which the heavy gear had been causing him. From his pink, smoking cranium came rivers of sweat, covering his bloodless, ghastly face. Bending forward to the clerk he whispered ceremoniously:

"Piccirilli Serafino."

.   .   .   .   .

The lawyer—thinking his morning work at an end—was tidying up his desk and making ready to go when he was faced by the three unknown clients:

"Who are you?" he said with bad grace.

"Piccirilli Serafino," the man breathed with a deep bow as he watched the two women curtseying to the ground as he had instructed them to do.

"Sit down," said the lawyer staring at the unusual clients, "but be quick as I am expected at lunch."

The three sat in a row facing the desk, fearfully embarrassed. Piccirilli tried to smile but his face was pitiful. Obviously he had forgotten how to smile.

"You see. . ." he began.

"We have come to ask . . ." broke in the daughter.

"Unbelievable things . . ." puffed the mother, her eyes glued to the ceiling.

"Speak one at a time," frowned the lawyer. "I told you I am in a hurry. What is it you want of me?"

"It's like this," said Piccirilli with a gulp. "We have been served with a summons."

"Murder, sir, murder," burst in the wife.

"Mama, please," said the daughter, trying to calm her.

Piccirilli looked at his wife and with as much authority as his miserable physique would allow he begged:

"Let me speak, Mararo."

Then turning to the lawyer:

"We have received a summons. We have been forced to leave the house we were occupying because . . ."

"I understand," broke in the lawyer. "Order to quit."

"No, sir," said Piccirilli apologetically. "Not at all; on the contrary it was we who left; we were forced to go even against the will of the land-lord. Now he claims damages for breach of contract and because he said we had given the house a bad name. . . ."

"But how?" said Zummo, his face darkening and turning this time to the wife. "You left the house, you have given the house a bad name and now the landlord. . . . Let's be clear; you can talk to a lawyer like to a priest. . . . Did you use the house for some immoral trade, for instance?"

"Certainly not," hurried Piccirilli, crossing both hands on his chest. "Nothing of the kind. No trade, whatever. We are not in business.

42

True, my wife lends from time to time a trifle of money . . . privately . . . at reasonable rate. . . ."

"I understand," said the lawyer, "the usual terms."

"Absolutely," confirmed the man; "terms of which even the Church would approve, but this has nothing to do with our case. Signor Granella —the landlord—says that we have defamed his house because during the three months we have lived in it we have seen strange things which make me shiver every time I think of them."

"May God ever prevent his worst sinners witnessing what we have seen," burst out the wife with a loud sigh, rising to her feet and making the sign of the cross.

"Persecution, a real persecution," muttered the daughter.

"Quite right, nothing else but persecution," added the father. "There is no other word. For three months we have been the victims of a persecution in that house."

"Persecution by whom?" yelled the lawyer, losing his patience.

"By . . . by ghosts," whispered Piccirilli after a long pause, leaning towards the desk and hiding

43

his mouth with his hand for fear of speaking too loud. "Yes, ghosts, sir."

"By whom? . . ." said the lawyer, thinking he had heard wrong.

"Ghosts, ghosts!" shouted the wife, waving her arm in defiance.

The lawyer jumped to his feet—furious.

"Nonsense—don't make me laugh! Persecuted by ghosts! Get out! Let me go to lunch, don't waste my time."

But the three, jumping from their chairs, drew nearer the desk, imploring:

"Don't go, don't go! You don't believe us, but we have seen them with our own eyes, we have seen them and heard them—they have persecuted us for three months."

They were all talking together, in an awful pandemonium which made the lawyer even more furious.

"Enough," he thundered, "you are crazy: you should see a specialist for mental diseases, not a lawyer."

"But I have been served with a writ," implored Piccirilli, his hands clasped as in prayer.

"Quite right too," shouted Zummo in his face.

"Is this your advice, then?" said the wife,

pushing the others aside. "Is this the way you deal with people needing help? You would not talk like this if you had been persecuted as we have been, if you had seen the ghosts as we have seen them."

"So you have really seen them, have you?" sneered the lawyer.

"Of course I have seen them," broke in the father. "With my own eyes."

"And I with mine," added the daughter.

"Yes, very likely with *those* eyes," exploded the lawyer, pointing at their squints.

"Then what about mine?" screamed the wife, stretching her right hand on her breast and opening her large black eyes as wide as she could. "These are straight, by God, and big enough to see! And they have seen those ghosts as clearly as they see you now."

"You are sure, are you?" said Zummo, mockingly.

"Quite sure," sighed the woman. "But if you still don't believe us we can produce witnesses, people who will come and tell what they have seen too. . . ."

The lawyer frowned, obviously impressed.

"Witnesses, you said?"

"Yes, sir, people who have seen and heard."

"Seen what, for instance?"

"Seen chairs moving about without anyone touching them."

"Chairs?"

"Yes, sir, chairs."

"What, ordinary chairs like the one in that corner?"

"Precisely, an ordinary chair going head-over-heels round the room like boys in the street and then—what shall I say—an orange-shaped pin-cushion made by my daughter being flung into the face of my husband as if thrown by an invisible hand. Oh! and a wardrobe trembling and squeaking as in a fit which from inside . . . from inside . . . (my flesh creeps at the mere thought of it). . . shouts of laughter would break through."

"Shouts of laughter," added the daughter.

"Shouts of laughter," confirmed the father.

But the wife, without losing time, went on.

"Dozens of neighbours have seen all this and would be ready to give evidence, as I told you, while we three have seen and heard even more."

"Tinina, the thimble," broke in the father.

"Yes," began the child with a sigh. "I had a little silver thimble, a present from my grandmother (God bless her soul!). I was terribly fond of the little thing, but one day it disappeared. I searched the whole house for three days and could not find it until, one night, as I was sleeping under my mosquito net. . . ."

"It's full of mosquitoes, too, that accursed house," broke in the mother.

"And what a size the mosquitoes are," confirmed the father, shaking his head.

"I heard the noise of something jumping on the roof of the net," continued the daughter.

"It was like a rubber ball bouncing from the floor," interrupted the father, stopping the child with a gesture.

"Then suddenly the small object, it was my thimble, was thrown violently against the ceiling and fell to the ground—dented!"

"Dented," confirmed the mother.

"Dented," repeated the father.

"I got out of bed, trembling, to pick it up, and just as I was bending down, from the ceiling came. . . ."

"Shouts of laughter, shouts and shouts of laughter . . ." ended the mother.

The lawyer stood silent for a while, his head bent and his hands behind his back.

"Playful ghosts!" he said after a while, scratching his head with a finger and trying to scrutinize the truth of this unbelievable tale. "Go on, go on; it's most amusing."

"Playful? Not playful at all, sir," retorted the woman. "Infernal, you mean. Ghosts that snatch the sheets from our beds, sit on our stomachs at night, clasp us by the shoulders, seize our arms, shake our furniture, ring the bells as if an earthquake had burst out, poison our food, throw ashes in the pans, is that your idea of playful? Not even the priest with his holy water could stop them; and when we told Granella d'you know what he had the cheek to answer? 'Nonsense, eat well and cure your nerves.' We begged him to come and see for himself but he would not listen. In fact, he even threatened us. 'Be careful how you talk or I'll finish you',—his very words."

"And he has finished us," concluded the husband bitterly. "Now, sir, we are in your hands. You can believe us. We are respectable people, and we shall know how to repay you."

The lawyer, as usual, pretended not to catch the last sentence. For a long while he stood by the desk, tugging at his moustache, deep in thought.

48

Then he looked at the clock. It was nearly one. His people had been waiting for him for almost an hour and his lunch was long overdue.

"It is a peculiar case," he said at last. "You quite understand that I cannot accept your story of the ghosts: all you said may be mere imagination . . . mere gossip . . . but I am considering the legal side of the question. You say you have seen . . . hm! I don't like the word ghost . . . you have seen something . . . we shall say—and you have witnesses to prove that it was impossible for you to continue to live in the house because of . . . er . . . of a kind of . . . shall we say . . . er . . . peculiar persecution. . . . I must agree the case is novel and interesting . . . I may feel inclined to take it on. . . . Perhaps it will be possible to find some legal argument in your favour. Let me think it over before I decide. It's late now, but if you call again to-morrow I will let you know what I can do for you!"

.　　　.　　　.　　　.　　　.

Almost unconsciously the thought of this strange case was turning and turning in the lawyer's mind like a windmill. At lunch he couldn't eat: after lunch—when he lay on the bed for a nap as he used to do during the summer months—he couldn't get to sleep.

"Ghosts," he would say to himself with a sneer, while the vision of the three comic figures who swore over and over again of having seen them was flashing back to his mind.

Many times as a child he had been told stories about ghosts which had terrified him and made him spend sleepless nights.

"The soul," he sighed, stretching up his arms beneath the mosquito net and letting them fall back heavily on the bed. "The soul . . . the immortal soul. . . ." Of course, to believe in ghosts, he admitted, one must believe in the immortality of the soul, it's obvious, but did he believe in it or not? He had always said that he didn't and how could he now admit even a doubt? Could he go back on his own belief? He knew that one often lied to oneself, that people are often afraid of exploring their own selves for fear of discovering that they are so different from those they believe themselves to be or from those for whom they want to be known. But how many had ever given a serious thought to the question of the soul? Life was so absorbing that one hardly had time to think over these matters; yet they should be more important than all others. A friend dies and—like obstinate animals—we refuse to think of him beyond the moment of death, fully satisfied with the recollection of the past, and merely lighting a cigar to dispel our distress. Even science, as it happens, does not go beyond human existence, ignoring death and refusing to consider it. "Do not worry about death"—says science—"carry on your daily duties, think of your present life, of your work, of your profession." Quite right. The lawyer, too, so far, had refused to be worried about death, but here it was: the immortal soul—or ghosts—as it happened, knocking at his door, forcing him to be bothered with them. "You want to ignore us" —they seemed to tell him. "You wanted to ignore death but here we come, from the kingdom of the dead knocking at the doors of those who are still alive, making fun of you, making chairs and tables dance round your room, frightening your clients, laughing at them from the depths of an old wardrobe, puzzling you to-day—my learned lawyer—and puzzling to-morrow a body of equally learned judges who will have to try the most novel action ever heard in any court, an action for damages against ghosts!" Could he still ignore them?

Jumping from his bed, full of excitement, Zummo went back to his study and to his books of reference.

Articles 1575 and 1577 of the Civil Code seemed to offer some ground for his case.

They laid down—"inter alias"—that the lessee of a house was entitled to the "peaceful enjoyment" of the property during the period of the lease and that "the lessor was responsible to him for any undisclosed nuisance which might reduce or hinder the full enjoyment of the tenancy."

The law was clear but—here was the crux of the case—it was necessary to prove the existence of ghosts and their presence in that house.

He had statements and witnesses to corroborate his clients' story, but to what extent was the evidence reliable? How could he quote scientists to substantiate these statements?

Having again questioned the Piccirilli family the lawyer promised to accept the case and to work on it with the best of his skill.

.   .   .   .   .

He first read a general history of spiritualism, from the origins of mythology to the present day; next he consulted Jacolliot's book on the wonders of fakirism; and he then read everything written on the matter by the greatest and most reliable experts, from Crookes to Wagner, from Aksafof to Gibier and Zoellner, from Janet to de Rochas, from Richet to Morselli. He thus learnt—much to his astonishment—that even the most sceptical men of science had declared that the so-called "spiritual phenomena" could not be put in doubt.

He was elated. "Now"—he said to himself— "things begin to look much brighter." So long as these phenomena had been reported by people of no importance, like the Piccirillis, he, a man of sound education and grounded in positive science, had a good right to laugh at them. Even if he had seen them with his own eyes he could have believed them to be the result of some hallucination. But when men of science like Lombroso or Richet had acknowledged their existence the matter was entirely different.

Forgetting his clients and his case, he gave himself up, with ever increasing conviction, to the study of spiritualism. For a long time his

past work—yet so flourishing and so remunera-
tive—had failed to give the intellectual satisfaction for which he had been craving. Lost in
that little town where so little could be found to
satisfy his hunger for the higher outlets of the
brain, he now found that a new opening had been
revealed to him by those books on the great
problem of the after-death. Could then the great
problem of death be solved? Could the soul of a
dead person come back for an instant and
"materialize"? Could it come back to him, who
had been so blind, shake his hand and say:
"Zummo, don't worry. Don't trouble about your
petty existence on earth. There is something else,
a much better life awaiting you one day!! Forward! Don't fear!"

Almost every day Piccirilli, either with his wife
or his daughter, was coming to see him and to
discuss the case.

"I am still working on the case: don't worry:
I am not forgetting you," the lawyer would say.
But, to tell the truth, he had completely forgotten
everyone, putting off as many cases as he could
and even refusing to interview new clients. At
last, however, out of gratitude to the poor
Piccirillis, who had unconsciously shown him the

way to light, he decided to go carefully into their case.

A grave difficulty met him at the very outset. In all experiments of which he had read, the presence of ghosts had been revealed through a medium. No doubt, then, one of the three Piccirillis—even without knowing it—must be a medium and—in this case—the nuisance of the ghosts was due to the tenants and not to the house. This would mean the collapse of the whole case. On the other hand why—if one of the Piccirillis was a medium—had the ghosts ceased to appear in the new home? Why had they never appeared in any of the houses where they had lived before? Obviously there must be something in the popular belief that ghosts only live in certain houses, and if this could be proved his case would stand. Furthermore, had not the witnesses corroborated his clients' statement? This alone should disprove the explanation given by some scientists that ghosts are only seen by certain persons. Medium or no medium—he thought—ghosts have their own existence and to make doubly sure he would call on the Piccirillis and find out the truth for himself by holding a séance and watching results.

Frightened at this suggestion the Piccirillis refused to have anything to do with the experiment, but the lawyer insisted that the test was useful—even essential—for the case, and a séance was held. Tinina was found at once to be a powerful medium and Zummo—mad with joy —was thus able to witness almost all those astonishing revelations of which, so far, he had only been acquainted through his book. The Piccirillis' case—it is true—was collapsing, but his own knowledge of the after-death was widening to such an extent that he could not help feeling mad with joy. "Let Granella win his case, my friends. . . . What does it matter? Don't you see that here, before us, stands the revelation of the immortal soul?"

But how could the Piccirillis share their lawyer's enthusiasm for the immortal soul? They thought he had gone mad. They refused to believe that these experiments were anything else but infernal practices of which they were the victims. They had escaped from Granella's ghosts to fall amongst their lawyer's demons. Could anything be worse? Was he going to ruin them for ever? That would be the result of the case if somebody got to know what was going on at their place.

"Don't be afraid," the lawyer would say contemptuously. "Do you take me for a babe? Here you see me as a friend, not as a lawyer. When the case will come for hearing, I shall know how to plead the mysterious nuisance of the house!"

.   .   .   .   .

And he did, in fact, plead that the nuisance was due to the house, not to the presence there of some extraordinary medium, but his pleadings were so unconvincing that his case was lost from the beginning.

On the contrary he amazed the court, his colleagues and the public with an unexpected and bombastic profession of faith, describing Allan Kardech as the "New Messiah," speaking of spiritualism as "The new religion of humanity," and showing how the tree of life had been practically dried up by science but was now likely to be revived under the warmth of new faith. "The mystery of death"—he said—"would soon be revealed: the veils of darkness would soon be lifted while quaint shadows are already creeping through the space to warn us about a world of beyond. . . ."

And here he proceeded to speak of the most astonishing phenomena of spiritualism with such dramatic eloquence that the audience—carried away by his words—was enthralled and spellbound. The court, however—more practically minded and less inclined to follow the lawyer in his sublime heights—refused to give a verdict for his clients. Modern science—they said—had not yet accepted the still uncertain theories arising out of spiritualism. Besides, how could the lessor be held responsible for ghosts, for wandering shadows with no material substance? And how could ghosts be called "undisclosed nuisances" as specified by the law? Besides, was not the control of ghosts beyond the physical power of man and, if so, how could the landlord be asked to be responsible for them? No, the court could not agree with the lawyer's brilliant defence, and "judgment for the plaintiff" was their only possible verdict.

The public—still crystallized by the amazing and absorbing defence—greeted the verdict with unmistakable signs of disapproval. The lawyer himself—unable to refrain a flood of indignation which almost caused his arrest—rushed out of the room dragging after him his three dismal clients whom he pointed out to the cheering crowd as the "martyrs of a new religion."

Across the piazza, Signor Granella—the owner of the house—stout and blustering—was watching the crowd, with his hands in his pockets, letting it be well heard by those round him that he would not be scared to spend the night alone in the haunted house. He would sleep there that very night alone—he said—without a servant, as the Piccirillis had so ruined the reputation of the house that not even his most trusted servant would accompany him. Yes, this was what the Piccirillis had done to him, he said. It had become a lost house, a house in ruins. But now that the court had given their judgment and restored the reputation of the house he would go there himself and sleep there alone, not afraid of facing those ridiculous ghosts.

Ah! Ah! He would have something to tell them if they ever dared to show themselves. . . .

. . . . .

Granella's house was built on the highest point of the town at the very top of the hill, not far from the "Gate of the Winds." It stood there alone, on a large open space only facing a ruined shed where an occasional carman would shelter for the night while keeping an eye on his mule and cart.

Only a grim oil lamp would provide a glimmer of light over the square on moonless nights, but a few yards below—on the other side of the gate— life would start again with its endless rows of thickly populated dwellings so that—although somewhat lonely and gloomy at night—it was an ideal residence with plenty of air and freedom, full with comforts which could seldom be found in other residences of the same town.

It had been fully re-papered and re-painted since the Piccirillis' departure. Granella had lavished money freely in cleaning it up from top to bottom, but although so many visitors had come to inspect it—perhaps out of curiosity—nobody had made an offer and no tenant had yet been found for it.

"Well," repeated Granella to those near him, "I'll sleep there to-night," and, having brought to the place an iron bedstead, a chest of drawers, a washing stand and a few chairs—enough to furnish one room—he kept to his word and walked to the house at dusk taking good care to let his neighbours know what he was doing.

"But why those two pistols?" commented the neighbours, watching the two large-sized fire-arms hanging at his belt.

If gangsters had threatened the house those pistols might have been useful but what use could firearms be against ghosts?

Was Granella afraid? Of course he was not; he had been laughing and sneering all through the trial and there was no reason to be afraid now; but somehow—a queer feeling—why had that confounded lawyer been talking so much about ghosts and spiritualism? Why had he been allowed to talk of "proofs" and of scientific backing, thus staggering the audience and allow-ing even respectable people to admit that there might be some truth, after all, in what he said? In fact, hadn't one of the judges even admitted to Zummo in confidence—immediately after the trial—that his speech had shattered his opinions and that it was only out of respect for the present state of legislation that he had to concur with the other judges in the verdict? It was that swaggering Zummo who—with his speech—had carried away the whole town and was now making him feel lonely and disgruntled as though his friends had let him down, like cowards.

A CHARACTER IN DISTRESS

There wasn't a soul on the wide ground upon which the house stood. How bare, how dismal the place looked. Even the tiny flame of the street lamp seemed to flicker and tremble as though frightened by the thick darkness of the surrounding valley. He let himself into the house. . . . Why was the flame of the candle fluttering as if someone were blowing on it? (It was his own excitement causing him to puff through his nostrils.)

Crossing several empty rooms to reach the one he had furnished, his eyes were glued on the flame which he sheltered with his hand to avoid seeing the shadow of his own body monstrously enlarged on the walls. The bed, the chest of drawers, the basin, the chairs, all seemed lost in the darkness of the room. He placed the candle on the chest of drawers and could go no further. His heart was pounding. He was bathed in sweat. . . . And now what next? He must bolt the door as he used to do at home; but before doing that why not try to open the window just a tiny bit and get out on the balcony? . . . It was so hot inside. The fresh paint was stinking. Yes, he would let some fresh air come in while he made up his bed. He took out a sheet from a bundle he had brought and laid it on the mattress. A knock seemed to come from the door. A shiver ran through his loins hitting him like the stroke of a razor. Who is it? A knob of his iron bed must have knocked against the wall. He waited, terrified. . . . Silence. Yet that silence, somehow, seemed alive. . . .

He pulled himself together and got hold of one of his pistols. Holding the candle in the other hand he pushed the door and shouted:

"Who's there?"

The echo of his voice in the empty rooms made him step back but he soon recovered, stamping his foot and pointing his pistol to the imaginary enemy.

"Who's there?"

Nothing. Silence. Charily he pushed the door a little wider. Nothing in the room but a ladder left behind by the decorator. No doubt the knock was due to the knob of the bed. He returned to his room and went out on the balcony.

"Shrr. . . ."

Curse that bat. It had been attracted by the light of the candle of course, and Granella laughed, watching the little animal flutter in the

63

darkness, but a new squeak from the bedroom made him jump again.

Nonsense, it was the newly pasted paper on the walls trying to make fun at him. He laughed again, but looking inside the room something terrible caught his eyes; an enormous white tongue stretching itself along the floor from the adjoining room.

Curse that roll of wallpaper left behind by the workmen on top of the steps and now unrolling itself through the door like a devil's tongue.

Granella had had enough. He shut the window and, seizing hat and candle, flew down the stairs. Not a soul outside the house. He carefully let himself out and sliding along the wall of the house he swiftly dwindled through the darkness into town.

A night in the open would do him good, he thought. After all, why risk his health for that wretched house?

He had been silly. It was a mistake to go there that night without first getting used to it. He would try again to-morrow night. . . .

But somebody had watched him in his flight from the house. A carman sheltered from the ruined shed had seen him creeping along the walls and had spoken to the neighbours who in their turn had informed the lawyer.

Zummo was thrilled.

"I knew it! I knew it!" he shouted, mad with joy. "I swear to you that I had foreseen all this. I knew that sooner or later Granella's own evidence would be in our favour. Now let's all work together and waste no time."

The trap was set for the same night. The lawyer and five or six trusted men—no more— would collect the evidence they required. Let them all hide in the shed and watch. Above all not a word to anyone, for God's sake.

"Swear."

"We swear."

No professional triumph in Zummo's career could have been greater than on that night when —after a long watch with his friends—he saw Granella, barefooted, shivering and terror-stricken, grasping his shoes in one hand, and holding with the other hand the trousers which he had not had time to button. He was creeping from the house, like a thief, trying to escape.

Springing from the shadow, Zummo was on him like a tiger.

"Good evening, Signor Granella. Enjoying a quiet walk, eh?"

It all happened in a flash: five or six men were round poor Granella laughing and sneering, pushing him against the wall.

"Now, old fool, do you believe in the immortal soul? Blind justice has given you the verdict, but who was right? Tell us, tell us, what did you see? ... Speak ... what did you see?"

It was all in vain, for poor Granella, crying and trembling, was unable to answer. He had simply lost his speech.

AN OVERSIGHT

BLACK amongst the glaring dust of a scorching August sun a third-class hearse drew up at the main entrance of one of the many new houses built in the popular district of Prati di Castello in Rome.

It was about three in the afternoon.

All those new houses, for the most part still tenantless, seemed to stare at that black hearse passing under their empty and still lifeless windows.

They had just been built to receive life and yet death was already preying upon them. Horrible! death before life.

The hearse had arrived slowly, almost crawling. The driver, half asleep on the box, a foot resting on the mudguard and his worn-out topper tipped on his nose, had stopped the hearse at the first door which he had seen ajar as a sign of mourning and had lain down on the box to have a more comfortable snooze.

A CHARACTER IN DISTRESS

From behind the door of the only shop, lifting the corner of a greasy canvas blind, a rough, hairy fellow had sprung shouting to the driver:

"Not here, old man . . . not here . . . further down. . . ."

The driver, looking at him from below the brim of his topper resting on the nose, released his brake and moved further on, passing in front of the shop, without saying a word.

Here or there, what did it matter to him?

And stopping at the next door which again seemed ajar in mourning he settled himself once more to sleep.

"Idiot," muttered the chemist, "he does not even know that every house leaves its main door ajar at this time of the summer. He must be a novice at his business."

So it was, in fact. Nor did Scalabrino have any special liking for his new job. He had been a house-porter and had quarrelled with his tenants and even with his own employer: he had been a sacristan and had quarrelled with his vicar: he had been a cabman and had quarrelled with the cab owners. This last quarrel had happened only three days ago and—unable to find a better job in that dead season—he had become a temporary hearse driver. He would quarrel even with the undertaker—he was quite sure of it—because the world was full of wrongs and besides hadn't the world always been unfair to him? It was enough to have a look at him. Hunched-up shoulders, bulging eyes, a lemon-coloured face, and a red nose like a cherry. Why was his nose so red? Was it to enable everyone to take him for a tippler while he didn't even know the taste of wine? He had enough of that filthy life. One day or another he would have a last quarrel, with the water of the river and—good-bye for ever.

Meanwhile here he was—half killed by flies and boredom—under the blazing sun waiting for his first load—a corpse.

And the corpse had emerged, after a good half-hour, but from an entirely different door, at the end of the road, on the opposite side.

"Hell with you . . ." he muttered, moving on with the hearse while the bearers, panting under the weight of a miserable-looking bier, were cursing at him.

"Idiot. Didn't they give you the number of the house?"

Scalabrino turned round the hearse without a

word so as to allow the men to lower the flap
and load their cargo.

"Ready," they shouted, and again resting his
foot on the mudguard and tipping his topper on
his nose, he moved slowly away for the cemetery.

Not a flower, not a ribbon on the bare hearse.

Behind walked a solitary mourner, a woman.
Her face was hidden by a thick black veil, she
was dressed in black muslin printed with heavy
yellow flowers and was carrying on her shoulder
a light coloured parasol to protect her from the
scorching sun.

She alone was following the hearse, her head
bent to the ground, more perhaps in shame than
in grief.

"Pleasant walk, Rosie," the hairy fellow of
the shop shouted with a snigger when she
passed his door.

The mourner turned round to look at him
through her veil: she waved to him with her
mittened hand, then lowered it again to hitch up
her skirt trailing on the ground, and showing two
horribly down-at-heel shoes.

"Poor Signor Bernardo," said a loud voice from
one of the windows, "they bury him like a dog."

"A famous professor with only a cook to mourn

him," retorted a woman's voice from another window.

Before reaching the main street Scalabrino turned his head round and feeling pity for that solitary mourner walking behind the hearse stopped his horses and suggested that she should engage a cab.

"You will tire yourself . . . it's a long way to the cemetery . . . you may get a sunstroke. . . ."

Rosie shook her head under the black veil. She had promised her master—the old professor— to follow his hearse at least half-way to the cemetery and she was not going to break a promise given on the point of death.

"But how would he know?" retorted Scalabrino.

"Impossible, quite impossible." Rosie would not hear of a cab.

"Not even if I paid your fare?" suggested Scalabrino, who at bottom was a man of good heart.

Not even then, not even if she had had to fall under the scorching sun of the hottest Roman summer would Rosie give way—and Scalabrino —chewing a blasphemy—continued his journey through the deserted streets of the capital, slowly, almost crawling towards the square of San Lorenzo where his mourner would allow him to proceed alone with his cargo to the main cemetery.

So far he had—although with great difficulty—managed to keep himself awake, thus avoiding the traffic, the electric trams and the motor-cars, none of which seemed to take notice of this miserable third-class hearse crawling along at that unusual hour of the day. But when—after having passed through the busiest part of the town—he reached the long winding road leading to the higher and less congested districts of the city he again tipped his hat on his nose, rested his foot on the mudguard and settled down to a fresh snooze.

The horses—he thought—are sure to know the way.

The few passers-by stopped to stare at him, indignant, and surprised. A driver was asleep on the box and a corpse was asleep in the coffin: one resting by the warm summer sun and the other lying lifeless in the cold shadow of darkness: behind them a solitary mourner with a black veil on her face and a light coloured parasol on her shoulder . . . could anything be more gruesome and yet comic than this queer, solitary, silent

procession at such burning hour of the day?
What bad taste for a man to be buried on a
suffocating day like that: what a lack of dignity
and self-respect. Was it to be wondered at, if the
driver had fallen asleep?

And how much better would it have been for
Scalabrino if he had continued to sleep until the
cemetery instead of waking up—as he did—at a
sudden jerk of his horses quickening their pace
when they reached the top of the hill.

And as he awoke he saw standing on the
pavement a tall, emaciated gentleman with
black whiskers and a pair of large dark spectacles
who threw at him a large parcel which hit his
face and almost knocked his topper from his head.

Before Scalabrino had had time to realize what
had happened the gentleman had already jumped
in front of the horses stopping them, shaking his
fists at Scalabrino as though—having nothing else
to throw—he was going to throw his hands at
him while screaming and yelling:

"Scoundrel, rascal, blackguard. Doing this
to a man like myself, to the father of eight
children . . . rascal, scoundrel. . . ."

A crowd soon gathered round the hearse:
passers-by, shop-keepers, tenants of the neigh-

bouring houses, people from the adjoining streets all rushed to see what had happened, each one enquiring from the others, all of them standing on their toes to have a better view.

"What is it?"

"A woman . . . they say . . . the driver. . . ."

"Somebody dead?"

"Yes."

"Where?"

"Inside the hearse."

"Who?"

"A professor."

"Will they arrest him?"

"Who, the dead?"

"No, the driver . . . it was his fault. . . ."

In the meantime the tall, emaciated gentleman with black moustaches and a pair of large dark spectacles had been dragged to a neighbouring café where he was still shouting and asking the return of the parcel he had flung at the driver, although nobody knew yet why he had thrown it.

On his box, Scalabrino, more lemon looking than ever, was replacing the topper on his head while answering the policeman who—surrounded by a vociferous crowd—was taking notes in his pocket-book.

AN OVERSIGHT

At last the hearse moved on again, opening up a narrow passage through the crowd, still followed by the solitary mourner half hidden behind the black veil and the light coloured umbrella.

There was a silence when the crowd saw her; only one or two urchins whistling a mild protest.

But what had happened, then?

Nothing: a mere oversight. Scalabrino—who had been a cab-driver up till three days before, had been so overtaken by the sudden awakening from his snooze, still half dazzled by the scorching sun, that he had completely forgotten he was driving a hearse. He had thought of being still driving a cab and following his old habit of nodding at people standing on the pavement he had nodded to the tall emaciated gentleman with the black moustaches and a pair of large dark spectacles whom he had seen standing by, making him the usual little sign with his finger:

"Fare wanted?"

Of course, it was a bad oversight, but what Scalabrino has never been able to understand is why, for such a small matter, the tall emaciated gentleman had made all that fuss.

THE HUSBAND'S REVENGE

FROM the very first day of his betrothal, Bartolino had heard his fiancée say to him:

"Lina, you know, is not my real name. It should be 'Carolina,' but 'Lina' was the name my beloved late husband gave me . . . and 'Lina' I have remained. He was such a good man . . . there he is . . ." and she had pointed to a large photograph showing Signor Cosimo Taddei, smiling and taking off his hat to him.

Bartolino, almost instinctively, had half bowed his head to the dead man in reply.

It had never occurred to Lina Sarulli, the widow of the famous architect Taddei, to remove his portrait from the wall, for to him she owed her position, the house he had built for her, the beautiful furniture and everything else she possessed in the world.

"I didn't really like to change my name," she had continued, oblivious of her fiancé's embarrassment. "But could I refuse what the dear soul asked me? I am sure you will not mind calling me by the same name, will you?"

"No . . . er . . . no . . . of course," Bartolino had stammered, unable to turn his eyes from the large photograph of the man on the wall who was still smiling and raising his hat to him.

.   .   .   .   .

When—three months later—friends and relatives had come to the station to see Lina and her bridegroom off for their honeymoon, Ortensia Motta, Lina's closest friend, had turned to her husband and had not been able to refrain from a sigh: "Poor Bartolino, with a woman like that. . . ."

"Why poor?" had answered her aged husband, who, having arranged the marriage, was annoyed at any criticism. "Why poor? Bartolino is not a fool, he has a first-rate knowledge of chemistry."

"Yes—of chemistry," had added the wife.

"And he will make an ideal husband, as he would have made an ideal teacher if he had cared to publish all he knows about chemistry. Besides, he is such a candid soul. . . ."

"I agree, a perfectly candid soul," said his wife, unable to conceal a smile while thinking of her friend Lina travelling at that very moment to Rome on her second honeymoon, with that bald, inexperienced, almost childish-looking young man replacing the delightful, jovial, shrewd and enterprising (even too much, at times) Signor Taddei who had been her first husband.

.   .   .   .   .

Before the train started Uncle Anselmo had said to the bride: "Take care of Bartolino. . . . Look after him."

And Lina—who had already been to Rome on her first honeymoon and knew all about travelling —had in fact taken care of him, like a child, and when the train at last reached Rome she had said to her husband: "Leave everything to me, dear"—and, turning to the porter who had collected the luggage: "To the Hotel Victoria."

Immediately outside the station the 'bus of the Hotel Victoria was waiting. Lina recognized the driver and gave him a nod.

"You will see, dear, a nice little hotel; clean, good service, not too expensive and quite central. . . . The same one I went to with my beloved six years ago for my first honeymoon. . . . You will like it too. . . ."

Arriving at the hotel Lina felt almost at home. Nobody seemed to know her but she was sure she could recognize everyone. There was "Pippo," for instance, the old waiter who attended "them" six years ago. He showed her room N.12—on the first floor—a large, well-furnished room, which, however, had not suited her.

"I wonder whether room nineteen is vacant, Pippo?" she had asked the old waiter, and while the servant had gone to enquire she had remembered that the same thing had happened to her beloved, six years ago. They had reserved for him a room on the first floor, but he had asked for another on the second, N. 19.

"We shall be better there, my dear; more air, less noise. . . . It is the same room. . . ."

And when Pippo had returned saying that N.19 was vacant she had clapped both hands like a child, happy to feel herself again in the same room, with the same furniture, with the same decorations, the same little alcove by the window.

Bartolino, of course, had not been able to share her joy.

"Don't you like it, dear?" she asked him.

And Bartolino, almost indifferent, had answered:

"I don't mind . . . provided you like it. . . ."

Then—while she had retired behind the little alcove—he had glanced at the bed. The same— he thought—where his wife had spent her first married night with Signor Taddei, her first husband. . . . And from far away, from the large photograph hanging at his wife's house, he could not help seeing before his eyes the vision of Signor Taddei smiling and taking off his hat to him.

.   .   .   .   .

While the whole honeymoon lasted not only did they sleep in the same bed but they took their meals at the same restaurants, they visited the same sights, the same museums, the same galleries, the same churches and even the same gardens as she had visited six years before—with her beloved husband. Bartolino—extremely shy by nature—was hardly capable of expressing his disgust in being forced to follow the experience, the advice, the taste and the personal likings of that first husband, nor did his wife notice the sad impression of her behaviour on her young husband. Married at eighteen, almost a child, ignorant of life and inexperienced, hadn't she been entirely formed and educated by that man so as to become his own creature? Didn't she owe everything to him and hadn't she become incapable of even thinking or feeling or moving apart from him?

If she had married again it was because Signor Taddei had taught her that tears are no remedy in life and that life is for the living and death for the dead. This—nothing else—had made her accept Bartolino as a husband. If Bartolino loved her he had to follow her in her own ways, which—of course—meant following the ideas of Signor Taddei who was their master and their guide.

But—thought Bartolino in the blind inexperience of his youth—why not at least some little thing, a kiss, for instance, a caress, something which might be different from what the other man had taught her? Something which might—even temporarily—take her away from the mastery of the dead man?

Yet his shyness prevented him even mentioning the idea or—less still—to revolt.

.　　　.　　　.　　　.　　　.

Upon their return from their honeymoon they were met by unexpected, sad news. Signor

Motta—the man who had arranged their marriage —had died suddenly.

Lina—who could not forget the support she had had from his wife Ortensia during her own widowhood, rushed to console and assist her, but could hardly understand why she looked so heartbroken although ten days had already elapsed since her husband's death.

"What can be wrong," she asked her husband.

"Well," answered Bartolino, blushing deep red at his wife's lack of understanding, "after all . . . hasn't she lost her husband?"

"Her husband? Of course, but he was old enough to be her father. . . ."

"And even then wouldn't that be enough to depress her?"

"But he was not her father . . ." insisted Lina.

Lina was right. Ortensia—who had noted how Lina's too frequent mentions of her dead husband had made Bartolino uneasy and restive, was trying to attract him by showing herself unconsolable and heartbroken. And by so doing she had impressed him so deeply by her sorrow that for the first time, blushing furiously, he had revolted to his wife.

"What about you? . . . Didn't you cry too? . . ."

"What has this got to do with it?" interrupted Lina. "First of all my beloved husband was. . . ."

"Still a young man, I know that," he finished to prevent her saying it.

"And besides I have cried . . . yes . . . cried quite a lot . . . but at last I have managed to control myself, while Ortensia does nothing else, just as if she would never think of stopping. . . . I am sure her tears are not sincere. . . ."

Bartolino, of course, would not believe this: on the contrary he felt more angry, not so much against his wife as against that dead husband of hers, the Signor Taddei, who was still smiling and raising his hat at him from the wall and whose way of thinking had obviously inspired and was still inspiring his wife.

That portrait! that everlasting smile! He could not stand it any more. It was haunting him, wherever he went, like a ghost. There it was, in front of him, laughing and taking his hat off to him as to say:

"It's your turn, make yourself at home. This was once my study as an architect: now it has become your laboratory as a chemist. Life is for the living, death for the dead. Work in peace."

Did he enter his bedroom? There too the image of Signor Taddei was pursuing him with his sinister smile as if to say:

"Come in, come in. Good evening. How do you like my wife? Did I train her well? Life is for the living, death for the dead."

No; he could stand it no longer. Every corner of that house was full of that man and Bartolino —the image of peace—had become restless and irritated, trying in vain to conceal his feelings from his wife.

At last he could conceal them no longer and tried to be eccentric so as to shake his wife's habits. But again he did not succeed.

"You behave just like my poor beloved," reproached his wife. "He was so extravagant, the dear old soul."

And soon Bartolino became aware that his wife was enjoying his eccentricities as they reminded her of the very man he was trying to make her forget.

At last a wretched scheme came to his mind.

As a matter of fact it was not so much the intention of deceiving his wife as of revenging himself on that man who had taken his wife away from him and was still keeping her away after his death. He believed—in his inexperienced mind—that this wicked idea was his own and hardly did he know that—on the contrary—it had been almost unconsciously suggested to him by Ortensia who had already tried many times in vain to take him away from his studies while he was still a bachelor.

It was—for the wicked Ortensia—almost a return match, to tell Bartolino now—in the most artful way—that she was terribly grieved at betraying such a dear friend as Lina but that her love for him was born much before Lina had ever met him . . . a love almost as unconquerable as Fate. . . .

What Fate had to do with the whole thing Bartolino never understood and in fact—in the blessed simplicity of his mind—he was rather disappointed, feeling almost defrauded, when he saw that his scheme had been so easily carried out. Left alone a few minutes in the bedroom of his dear old friend Motta he soon was full of remorse. Suddenly his eyes fell on a shining object on the floor by Ortensia's bed. It was a small gold locket which had obviously slipped from her neck. He picked it up with the idea of handing it back to her, but, while he was waiting for her return, his nervous fingers had—unwittingly—opened it.

He could hardly believe his own eyes.

From that locket a tiny reproduction of a photo emerged: it was the same portrait of Signor Cosimo Taddei, who, raising his hat as usual, was smiling at him.

A WRONGED HUSBAND

WHEN civilization—still behind-times—compels a man to carry round his neck a long ladder from one lamp-post to another and climb up and down this ladder three times a day to fill up the lamps with paraffin, light them and put them out again, it is obvious that this man—even if dull and prone to drink—must eventually begin to talk to himself and push the height of his thoughts at least at the same level as his ladder.

Tonio—the lamp-lighter of Troni (in Sicily)—even fell from that height, one night, when drunk. He cut open his head and broke a leg. Only by a miracle he escaped death and after two months spent in hospital he went back to his work, his ladder round his neck with a leg shorter than the other and a heavy scar across his forehead. Yet each time he climbs up the ladder he cannot help resenting that the world should be so made as to compel a man to take notice of things which he would be so pleased to ignore. For instance, a husband may well be totally indifferent to his wife's unfaithfulness, but the world takes care that he should not be allowed to ignore it and even if he persists in taking no notice there will be plenty of people round him, even children, ready to remind him of it.

"How's your wife? Who is her best friend?" they shout when he is right at the top of the ladder lighting up his first lamps.

"Hell with you," he answers back. "Why come and tell me that now when I am just starting to light up the town? Can't you mind your own business and allow a decent fellow to earn his bread and butter?"

In fact—Tonio thinks from the top of his ladder—is it his fault if lamp-lighting allows no time to watch his wife? How can he bother about his wife when he has to climb his ladder three times a day to put right the endless lamp-posts of the town?

Yet, feeling the joke has now lasted too long, he had gone one day to the Town Hall to ask for advice. He had been received by Count Bissi, one of the Councillors, to whose influence he owed his job and also some occasional allowances as a reward for the faultless way in which the street lighting was being carried out under his care.

What Tonio wanted to know from "His Excellency" was whether when he is attending to the street lamps he could be considered as an official of the city.

"Yes, of course," answered the Councillor.

"Therefore whoever insults me insults an official of the city?"

"Not quite so," answered the Councillor, trying to prove that private matters have nothing to do with official duties, and that insults addressed to him as a husband cannot legally be said to be addressed to him as a lamp-lighter.

"Your Excellency knows best, of course, but if they insult me when I am lighting the town, when I am on the top of the ladder leaning against the lamp-post striking my match against the wall to light the wick, when they know that I cannot leave the city in darkness and run home to watch my wife and, if necessary, split open her head and that of her lover, what can I do? What would Your Excellency do in my place?"

He underlines the words "split open her head and that of her lover," for he knows that, as a wronged husband, the world imposes upon him even the unpleasant duty of becoming a murderer in order to avenge his honour.

"His Excellency" really finds it hard to give any advice.

"Does Your Excellency want another proof? On moonlight nights, when lamps are not lit, nobody ever mentions my wife to me. Why? Because they know that on those nights I cease to be an official of the city. I believe that something should be done, Your Excellency, and the police be informed. . . ."

Tonio's argument is right but it little matters. What matters, says "His Excellency," are the facts and the facts are that if Tonio seriously objects to being so insulted, if he believes that his wife's unfaithfulness is caused by his job as a lamp-lighter, then the best thing to do is for him to give up his job. If, on the contrary, he does not want to resign, he must take no notice of what the people say and carry on.

"Is this definite, Your Excellency?"

"Quite definite, I'm afraid," answers Count Bissi.

Tonio stands to attention with a military salute:

"Perhaps Your Excellency is right: I'd better keep the job."

.　　.　　.　　.　　.

A WRONGED HUSBAND

Each day the ladder seems heavier to the lamp-lighter and each day, dragging his shorter leg on its half-worn rungs, he finds his job more painful and tiring.

At times when he reaches one of the last lamp-posts on the narrow lanes at the top of the hill he stops lingering on the ladder, as though looking out from a window, almost hanging from his armpits to the bracket of the lamp, his hands swinging loose, his head resting on a shoulder. From there, forgetting his work and the advice of "His Excellency" thousands of thoughts come to his mind.

Strange, sad things, at times.

He thinks, for instance, that the stars, although so plentiful and so bright, do not even manage to light up the earth. What a waste.

Yet what a splendid sight a star-lit sky can be. He had once dreamt that he had been given the job of lighting up every star in the sky and he had tried to use a ladder so high that he could not see the end of it and so heavy that he could hardly hold it in his hands. What a terrible nightmare, that night, when he felt that it would have been impossible for him to reach the sky. A dream, of course, merely a dream, but how distressing and terrifying.

93

And how sad a lamp-lighter's job can be, he thinks. By providing light, he argues, he is also creating shadows, for nothing exists without its opposite. Death follows life and shadow is like death, following the body in all its movements. "People think I am giving them light, yet it's death which follows them when my lights begin to burn," he thinks, watching the shadows of casual passers-by from the top of the ladder.

But after all, concludes Tonio to console himself, his job is one of utmost importance because it makes good a failing in nature, the failing of light. He hates boasting but isn't he for this town the substitute of the sun? There are two substitutes, himself and the moon and they take it in turns. When the moon is there he rests: when the moon rests he works. And who would deny the importance of his job when the moon should be at work but fails to appear because clouds hide her and make her fail in her duty?

How lovely it is to watch in a moonless night a distant village lit up amongst the darkness of the surrounding country.

Tonio sees many of them each night when he reaches the last lamp at the top of the hill and stops to watch them at length, with his hands dangling from the bracket of the lamp and his head resting on a shoulder.

Similar to a multitude of glow-worms in council, those tiny lights stay on all night watching over the houses and the streets, inspiring a feeling of fresh hope and comfort in the midst of so much darkness. Every now and then a gust of wind blows past in the dark and all those tiny lights grouped together flicker and seem to sigh too.

Watching them from afar it looks as if all mortals, lost as they are on earth, had collected together to help and comfort each other. And yet it isn't so. If a house springs up in one place another does not spring up at its side, like a good sister, but opposite—like an enemy—blocking its view. And men too do not come together in order to keep each other company, but they prefer to encamp against each other for war. All this Tonio knows well. He knows that there is war in almost every house, war amongst those who should love each other and stand together against the rest. Isn't there war in his own home? Isn't his own wife—for instance—his worst enemy? If Tonio has taken to drink why has he done it?

Wasn't it because it helped him to forget and to ignore what was going on under his own roof?

.　　　.　　　.　　　.　　　.

But what is he doing? Doesn't he know there is no paraffin to-night in his lamps?

The town will have to remain in darkness. The lighting contractor has brought an action against the Council and the Council has stopped further payments with the result that the contractor, in his turn, has refused to supply further paraffin. Tonio has not been able to refill the lamps: he has merely gone round at dusk with his ladder trying to light them up with the little paraffin left from the previous night, but they burn for a bit and then go off with a stinking smell. The whole city is up in arms against him as if it were his fault.

"You better go home, Tonio. Who is your wife's best friend?" shout the urchins. Tonio cannot stand it any longer. The uproar increases; "Leave the lamp alone: it's your wife, not the lamps, that need watching."

And the uproar becomes worse. Tonio is furious. He leaves the main street and still carrying his ladder round his neck he seeks refuge in one of the narrow climbing lanes at the back. Yet many of the crowd still follow him. He pretends not to hear them and props his ladder on a lamp-post, but they are still shouting: "Your wife, your wife, who is her best friend?" Then, when tired and downhearted, he abandons himself on the bracket of the lamp, hoping the crowd will disperse, someone seizes the ladder from under his feet, leaving him there hanging from the armpits, kicking in the air like a puppet.

Tears come to his eyes. What on earth do they want from him? What have his domestic troubles to do with them? Do they want him to become a murderer because to-night there isn't sufficient paraffin in the city to light up the street lamps? If this is what they want, if they really think that he should carry out a duty on which he is not keen, let them bring back the ladder and he would show them how Tonio the lamp-lighter can split open the head of his wife and her lover.

Three or four of the crowd brought back the ladder under his feet and Tonio, his eyes burning with revenge, is soon down in the street making for home.

"Have you the big knife, Othello?" shouts one of the crowd.

"Of course I have it. Here it is."

He shows a huge hunting knife bulging from his pocket.

"Good enough to kill a bull, I swear by the Madonna."

"Will you kill them both?"

"Yes, both of them, like two pigs. Come and watch me. Follow me. Come and see."

And he hurls himself ahead dragging heavily through the narrow dark lanes, followed by the crowd.

"Do you really mean it then, Othello?"

Tonio stops, turns round and seizes one of his mockers by an arm:

"Do you think Tonio goes back on his word? Who do you think I am? Are you frightened then? Do you think Tonio is a coward? Come, follow me, all of you, you must see how Tonio can deal with an unfaithful wife and her lover."

And after a good shake to the man he has seized, he moves again towards home. Many of the crowd, feeling uneasy and frightened, follow him a few more steps, then they gradually stay behind and quietly slip away. Only four of them and a couple of urchins follow him to his home, this time no longer to watch a murder but anxious to avoid a real tragedy. In fact, as soon as he reaches the door of his house they take him by the arms and try to persuade him to join them in a drink. But Tonio wild with anger, panting, frees himself and threatens them with his knife: he kicks at the door and shouts to his wife:

"Open, open the door, filthy woman, open, I say. You are going to pay for all, this time."

In vain those of the crowd try to keep him back.

"Leave me alone," he shouts, "or I'll murder you too."

At this threat they all stand aside leaving him free to pull out a key from the pocket of his coat, open the door and run inside, banging the door back with a loud bang. Almost instinctively the crowd hurl themselves again, many of them shouting for help while tearing shrieks are heard from inside.

"Murder, murder," shouts Tonio, brandishing his knife in his hand after seizing his wife by the hair and throwing her on the floor in a half-dressed condition. Then he proceeds to look under the bed, in a linen chest, in the kitchen, all over the house, always shouting:

"Speak, speak, where have you hidden him?"

"Are you mad? Are you drunk?"

Down in the street the crowd has grown bigger: windows open here and there and everybody is asking:

"Who is it? What has happened? Will he murder her?"

And blows and kicks and shoves against the door.

Tonio bounds on his wife again:

"Tell me where he is or I'll kill you. Blood, blood. There will be blood to-night. Where is he? Speak."

He does not know where else to look. Then suddenly his eyes turn to a kitchen window which is never opened and its shutters are black with soot.

"Take a chair and open that window," he orders. And as she hesitates: "Very well, then, if you don't want to open it I'll do it for you."

He climbs on a stool and opens it. . . . Horror, Tonio stands back, his eyes petrified, his hands in his bristling hair. The knife drops from his hand.

Up there, almost hanging in the void, stands Count Bissi.

"Your Excellency . . . here . . . on this precipice. . . . You might have killed yourself. . . .

PUBLIC LIBRARY,
RAWTENSTALL.

Put a foot on my shoulder, Your Excellency . . .
be careful . . . mind you don't slip."

And turning to his wife, after landing a heavy
blow on her face:

"Can you imagine hiding 'His Excellency' on
that window with a risk of murdering him?
Didn't you have a cleaner place where to hide
him? Give me a brush, quickly, that I may dust
'His Excellency's' coat. Didn't you see that
I looked everywhere except in the wall cabinet
where a man could hide himself without the risk
of breaking his neck? Can a woman be such an
idiot?

"Let me brush you, 'Your Excellency.' How
could I have known you were there? Fancy your
standing outside that window over the precipice.
Would 'Your Excellency' oblige me by stepping
inside that wall cabinet only for a few minutes
until I run down and keep the crowd quiet?
Can you hear them shouting? They will ruin you,
'Your Excellency' if they find you here. . . . I
am sorry this has happened, but what else could
I do? There are certain duties one must perform
even against one's will. A few minutes only,
'Your Excellency,' inside that cabinet. . . .
They will soon go away."

And after having locked the Count inside the cabinet he rushes to the bedroom window open on the street, where the crowd is still shouting.

"You fools, did you really think there was going to be a murder? The house is empty: my wife was here alone. Come up and see for yourselves, if you don't believe me, but I assure you we are quite alone, my wife and myself."

SICILIAN HONOUR

As soon as prisoner Saru Argentu—known to his friends as Tarara—was brought into the caged dock of the squalid Court of Assizes he pulled out of his pocket an immense red cotton handkerchief heavily over-printed with yellow flowers and spread it with great care on the bench so as not to dirty the sky-blue coloured suit which he had bought specially for his trial. A brand new suit and a brand new handkerchief they were.

Then—sitting on the bench—he quietly turned his smiling face to the peasants packing the part of the Court left open to the public. His flat, fierce-looking face, freshly shaven but wrinkled and angular, with two heavy golden pendants dangling from his ears, gave him the peculiar appearance of a monkey which could not help being comic even in the sad atmosphere of a Sicilian Court.

A thick, horrid stench, a mixture of stable and

perspiration, a stink of goats, a fustiness of filthy animals, was filling the room.

Some of the women, shading their eyes with black mantillas, could not help crying at the sight of the prisoner, but Tarara himself, craning his neck right and left, went on smiling from his cage, now lifting one of his heavy rough hands as a salute, now nodding at them as if he were pleased to see again so many familiar faces of friends and work companions.

It was, in fact, almost a joy for him to be at last able to appear at his trial after so many months of preventive prison. He was so poor that he had not even been able to pay for a counsel of his own choice, and he had to accept legal aid of the State; but, as far as his own person was concerned, he had at least been able to come to the trial in a new suit, well groomed and freshly shaven as on a Sunday.

After the first formalities, the jury sworn in, the President ordered the prisoner to stand.

"Your name?"

"Tarara."

"This is a nickname. What's your real name?"

"Well, yes. . . . Argentu, Saru Argentu, Your Honour, but they all know me as 'Tarara'."

"Very well. How old are you?"

"I don't know, Your Honour."

"What, you don't know your own age?"

Tarara shrugged his shoulders, meaning that the question of age was a mere worldly vanity to which no one need attach too much importance.

"I live in the country, Your Honour. Who bothers about age, there?"

A burst of laughter filled the Court, and the President, bending his head, began to consult the papers in front of him.

"You were born in 1873: you are therefore thirty-nine."

Tarara opened both arms as if bending to the inevitable.

"Your Honour knows best."

To prevent fresh laughter, the President avoided putting more formal questions by giving himself the answer: "It is so. . . . It is so. . . ." At last he said:

"Sit down. The Clerk will now read you the charge for which you are being tried."

The Clerk started reading the charge, but he had soon to stop, for the foreman of the jury, overpowered by the stench of the Court, was on the point of fainting. Orders were given for all windows and doors to be left open.

It was then that the prisoner's superiority over those who were going to be his judges appeared as clear and as unquestionable as daylight.

.   .   .   .   .

Sitting on his huge scarlet handkerchief, Tarara was entirely indifferent to that nasty stench with which he was so familiar. He could in fact still smile, hardly feeling the heat in his heavy sky-blue Sunday suit. Even the flies—which were upsetting the members of the jury, the public prosecutor, the clerk, the lawyers, the ushers and even the gaolers—were not giving him the slightest trouble.

They were resting on his hands, buzzing round his face, sticking to his forehead or even to the corners of his mouth and eyes, but he was not feeling them, nor was he even trying to chase them away. Unconcerned with all this, he was all smiles for his friends. He was sure of his acquittal. He had murdered to defend his honour.

The young barrister briefed by the State for his defence had reassured him that although he was guilty of having murdered his wife, there could be no verdict of guilty, the murder indisputably having been committed on the discovery of her unfaithfulness.

In the blessed unawareness of the beasts, Tarara could therefore ignore even the remotest shadow of remorse. All that was puzzling him was the fact that he had been brought to answer for something which, after all, was no concern of anyone else but himself. All this staging of justice appeared to him as something inevitable, like Fate. Justice was for him like a bad year on land, nothing more. And justice, with all its solemn setting of high benches, bells, robes and uniforms was for Tarara something as mysterious as the great new steam mill of his village which had been opened with great pomp the previous year. One could bring his own grist to that mill, but who could guarantee that the flour one received back was from the same grist? It was a question of accepting with blind eyes and with resignation the flour which it pleased the miller to give.

Comparing the mysterious machinery of the steam mill (which had aroused in him so much diffidence) with the equally complicated and mysterious wheels of justice, Tarara could not help thinking that his case was like the grist brought to the mill: one had to accept the result which would come out of the trial as one had to accept the flour which came out of the mill.

He knew, of course, that he had split open his wife's head with a hatchet because, returning home on a Saturday night soaking with rain and covered with mud, he had found the whole lane astir over a horrible scandal which had broken out in his home. A few hours previously his wife had been discovered in his bedroom with the young Count Agatino Fiorica, the wealthy land-owner. It was Fiorica's wife who had informed the police and who had caused the two lovers to be arrested according to the law. It had become impossible for the neighbours to hide the event from Tarara, for his wife had been kept at the police station all night with her lover and next morning, when Tarara saw her creeping back to his door, he had leapt on her holding the hatchet in his hand and splitting her head before anybody had time to stop him.

All this he knew, of course, but how different it seemed from that long story which the Clerk was reading. . . .

.   .   .   .

When the Clerk finished, the President asked the prisoner to stand again:

"Prisoner at the bar, you have now heard the crime with which you are charged."

Tarara made a slight gesture and with his usual smile he answered:

"To tell you the truth, Your Honour, I did not pay any attention."

The President looked at him sternly:

"You are accused of having wilfully murdered with a hatchet your wife, Rosaria Femminella, on the morning of the 10th of December, 1911. What have you to say in your defence? Turn to the jury and speak to them clearly and with the respect due to justice."

Tarara laid a hand on his chest to convey his respect due to justice, but feeling that another burst of laughter might follow his words, he stood silent for a long time unable to find his words, uncertain and shy.

"Well," insisted the President, "what have you to say? Tell the jury all you know. . . ."

Tarara shrugged his shoulders and said:

"Your Honour and you, too, gentlemen, you are learned people who understood all that is written in those papers, but I live in the country.

If the writing in those papers says that I have killed my wife, then it is true and let us talk no more about it."

Even the President this time had to join in the general laughter.

"Let us talk no more about it? I am afraid you will soon see that there will be a lot to talk about, on the contrary."

"I mean, Your Honour," explained Tarara, again laying his hand on his chest, "I mean to say that I did it. Yes, I did it, that's all. I did it because I couldn't help it."

"Order, order," shouted the President at the fresh outburst of laughter, furiously ringing his bell. "This is a Court of Justice, where a man is being tried for murder. I shall order to clear the Court if there is more laughter and I must warn the jury on the seriousness of their task."

Then turning sternly to the dock:

"What do you mean by saying you could not help it?"

"I mean, Your Honour, that it wasn't my fault."

"Not your fault? Whose fault then?"

"Allow me to interrupt, Your Honour." The young State counsel jumped up, getting alarmed at the aggressive tone of the President. "It is quite obvious that if we carry on like this we shall be entangling this poor man altogether. I think he is right in saying that the fault was not his but that of his wife, who was betraying him with Count Fiorica. It's as clear as daylight."

"Let the prisoner answer for himself," rebuked the President. Then, turning to Tarara: "Is this what you intended saying?"

Tarara first shook his head, then added:

"No, Your Honour. It wasn't that poor woman's fault either. It was all the fault of that lady, Count Fiorica's wife, who stirred matters up. What business had she, I am asking Your Honour, that woman to raise such a terrible scandal at my doorstep that even the stones of the street had to blush for shame? What business had she to follow that perfect gentleman Count Fiorica to the slum of a dirty peasant? God alone knows, Your Honour, what we poor people have to do to earn a crust of bread."

.   .   .   .   .

There were tears in his eyes, while he was clasping both hands on his chest, but all round the Court people were bending in convulsions of

laughter. The President alone—and Tarara's
Counsel—had seen the importance of a statement
which seemed to rob the defence of its principal
argument: intense provocation.

"You confess, then?" said the President, "that
you were aware of your wife's relations with
Count Fiorica. Is it so?"

"Your Honour," interrupted the young
counsel, jumping to his feet, "I protest. This
question should have never been put. I formally
object to it being put to my client."

"But I am following your client's own confession . . ." retorted the President.

"My client has never confessed. All he said
is that the cause of his action was Signora Fiorica
raising such a scandal on his doorstep. . . ."

"Quite right, but you cannot stop me asking
the prisoner whether he knew before the day of
the crime of the immoral relations of his wife with
the Count."

The whole Court was getting restless. From
every corner violent signs were made to Tarara
that he should deny any knowledge of his wife's
unfaithfulness, but Tarara remained shy, uncertain
and frightened. He could find no words to
answer, turning at times to his counsel and at

times to the audience where dozens of hands
were making frantic signs of denial.

"Must I. . . . Must I . . . say no?" he muttered
to the audience.

"Old turnip," yelled somebody from the
bottom of the Court.

"You must tell the truth," admonished the
President. "In your own interest."

"Well, Your Honour, I am telling the truth,"
said Tarara, trembling and crossing both hands
on his chest. "I am. And the truth is this: I
knew it and yet it was as if I didn't know it.
The thing, Your Honour, was on the quiet and
nobody could have dared to face me and tell me
that I knew it. I am a peasant, gentlemen, and
what can a peasant know when he toils like a
beast in the fields from Monday morning till
Saturday night? What does a peasant know of
his troubles at home? Of course, if somebody had
come to me and told me: 'Tarara, your wife and
Count Fiorica are too friendly,' I would have
rushed home and split my wife's head with my
hatchet. But nobody had ever come to tell me,
Your Honour, and in order not to raise trouble I
even sent someone to give warning when I had
to return home earlier than the end of the week.

This shows, Your Honour, how careful I have been to avoid doing any harm to anybody. Men are what they are and women too. Of course men should know that women have it in their blood to be untrue even if their husband is never away, but women too should know that men cannot so lightly stand the scorn of their friends. . . . There are certain insults which slash your face like a knife. . . . No man can stand them. Now, gentlemen of the jury, you will understand me when I say that my poor wife would have never allowed me to be insulted, and in fact I have never even had a cross word with her, as all my neighbours can witness. But what fault have I, gentlemen of the jury, if that blessed lady, without any warning. . . . Yes, Your Honour, you should get her here, that lady, to face me and I would tell her: If your husband had had a similar affair with a spinster you might have pleased yourself as there was no husband to consider, but by what right have you come to upset me, who have always led a quiet life, who had nothing to do with the matter, who had always refused to see or hear anything, toiling from Monday morning to Saturday night in the fields to earn a living? Do you think you can allow yourself such fun? This scandal may be merely a joke for you: you are sure to take your husband back after a couple of days. But did it ever occur to you that your joke might affect the whole life of another man and that this man could not allow his face to be slashed by the ridicule you aroused and that he would have to act as a man must act? Why didn't you come to me first? I would have told you: Leave them alone. All men are alike. Man is a hunter. Can you really be jealous of a dirty peasant woman? Can you blame your husband if he fancies a bit of brown bread every now and then instead of the white one of every day? This, Your Honour, I would have told the lady and most likely nothing would have happened of what has happened through her fault, as I told you before, through her fault alone. . . ."

Hilarity mixed with loud comments followed the prisoner's long speech. With resounding ringings of the bell the President tried to restore order. Then he said:

"Prisoner at the bar. Is this your defence?"

"No, Your Honour, it is not my defence . . . it is the truth, merely the truth."

But as truth—even so candidly confessed—is not always easy to be accepted, the jury found Tarara guilty of murder with only mild provocation and a sentence of thirteen years' imprisonment followed.

MOTHER

"Traffic in children," said the charge, but there need have been no trial at all had it not been for the impulsive feelings of a woman for a baby.

Of course, you will say, if a married couple have no children of their own why don't they acquire one legally, by adoption, instead of doing what these two people did? Well, in their case, adoption would have been perfectly useless, for the husband had to prove that within ten years from the death of his aunt he had become the father of an heir, a child of his own, "born in legitimate wedlock," as the lawyer had put it. Yes, there was the will and nothing could alter it. The whole fortune, and it was a large one, would devolve to a benevolent society unless the birth took place within the ten years and not a day later. Thus the acid old spinster had decreed with gleeful anticipation of the torture and anxiety this condition would cause to her nephew.

The nephew had at once done his best to put

himself in a position to secure his aunt's large inheritance. Without waiting for the usual time of mourning to elapse he had set his eyes on what he thought the most suitable bride and had sought the doctor's advice.

The girl had, said the doctor, all the "physical guarantees": youth, health, a perfectly sound and well-developed body, everything to make an ideal wife and mother.

They were married. But, alas! even doctors go wrong at times, and in this case all anticipation seemed to have been utterly wrong. The first year, of course, the couple had treated the matter lightly, the second year they had grown more concerned and by the end of the fifth year the position between them had become so strained that endless quarrels and daily reproaches almost completely overshadowed the early happiness.

"It's your fault," the husband would say.

"It is entirely yours," the wife would retort with equal assurance.

The bickering was beginning to take a serious turn when one morning the wife bashfully confessed to her husband (all women are bashful when they speak of certain matters) that she believed the arrival of a baby in sight. The husband was half mad with joy. "A son! A son!" he went round shouting to his friends and relatives and all who cared to listen. "We shall have an heir at last!" and he almost gave orders to beflag his balcony with the large flag used for national events.

But, suddenly, when things seemed to be going on so happily and smoothly, something happened which you can better imagine than I can write, one of those unhappy events or phenomena—as doctors say—which, although rare, happen at times. Have you ever seen one of those beautiful balloons which children love to blow up and which deflate with a shriek as soon as their little finger is removed from the pipe? The same happened to that woman, with the exception of the shriek. The son and heir fizzled away in the air and she was left to mourn him.

Imagine the disappointment of the poor man and his dismay in having to announce it to all those to whom he had so proudly boasted his forthcoming paternity. The second time—for the same thing happened again—nobody knew of it and he kept his sorrow to himself, but the third time. . . . No, he did not wait for a third time, for, in the meantime, something happened, something entirely unforeseen, something so totally unexpected that it almost looked to be an inspired message from God sent to him as a consolation for his past sufferings.

He was sitting at home when a visitor was announced. It was an elderly woman, a nurse, the same nurse who had assisted his wife the first time.

"You see, sir, it happens like this. There is a young girl—her name wouldn't interest you—only seventeen. She came to see me: she is in trouble: of course I told her I would never agree to anything wrong . . . but she is in despair . . . she talks of suicide . . . the man is too poor to marry her. Her mother would kill her if she knew. . . . She is a servant girl, a nice young girl and I thought. . . . Perhaps you and your wife. . . ."

And to the benefit of all concerned it was arranged like this: the young girl was to keep the matter strictly secret even from her own mother: she was to enter the service of a lady who was "expecting a child" (this fact was to be widely advertised to all relatives and friends); the lady was to retire to a quiet home in the country with her maid so that, when the time came, the maid's child could be smuggled into her mistress's room and fill the empty cradle that awaited the long-expected heir.

There was nothing wrong in the scheme, they all thought, for after all, the unwanted baby would find a comfortable home among those who wanted him and, as far as the nurse was concerned she could at least claim the satisfaction, so rare in her profession where thousands of babies are brought into a world of poverty and unhappiness, of taking a baby from a nest of thorns and putting it in a bed of roses, of changing it from a poor and unwanted baby to a rich and most welcome heir.

But things went even better than planned, for the husband, not satisfied with having saved the young girl from suicide and dishonour, had also made her a present of twenty-five thousand lire ("a mere trifle compared with the amount of the expected inheritance"—his friends commented at the trial) as a dowry to enable her to marry the father of her child and to bear him as many children as he might ever want to have.

Everything had gone on smoothly and happily: the marriage of the young couple and the payment of the dowry immediately after the birth of the child: the perfectly kept secret of the girl's condition and of her baby's registration as her mistress's baby: the frequent trips to town of the husband bringing the good news of the forthcoming event and at last the wire announcing the heir's arrival in the world, which secured the large inheritance for ever.

But, when everything seemed so nicely settled, something happened at the last moment to change general happiness into consternation and ruin. It was all due to the wife's pity for that little baby, for that little mouth craving with hunger in her arms, while in the room above the healthy young mother could give it the sustenance for which it yearned.

It had been arranged that the mother would never see her baby. He was to be taken immediately to town where a wet nurse was ready for him. But at the last moment the wife took pity on the baby and thinking that no other woman could rear him better than his mother she herself took the little one to her and put him to her breast. That was the origin of all the trouble.

It was then arranged that they should all return to town together, the maid introduced to the relatives as the child's nurse. But nature asserted itself against all this scheming. When the young mother felt those two little hands clasping her breast and the little mouth avidly feeding itself, when she grasped for the first time in her arms the little creature to which she had given birth through so much anxiety and pain, the whole scheme seemed to her inhuman and impossible.

Yes, she had signed an agreement, she had received the money, she had of her own will allowed the child to be registered under another name . . . all this was criminal, there would be a charge against her as well, there would be a trial, there would be prison, but let the trial come, let the prison come, let everything come if she could have her son: the boy was her own and prison or no prison she was not going to allow anyone to take him away.

So it happened that they were all taken into custody and sent for trial: the nephew, his wife, the nurse, the young husband, his wife and, of course, her baby with her, all of them charged with one or more counts.

It was all in vain. The anxiety gave the poor young mother such a shock that the spring of life in her dried up, the child died after the first week and they were all left—like salt statues—with empty hands to await the result of their trial.

A WIDOW'S DILEMMA

When Signora Zorzi—clothed in the blackest of widow's weeds—paid her first visit to her husband's grave, she was escorted by Signor Gattica, himself a widower and an old friend of the deceased.

Each of them was carrying a large bunch of flowers: she for her husband and he for his wife. Solemn and composed, each holding the flowers in their hand, they paced mournfully towards the Pincetto—the highest corner of Rome's cemetery.

It was on that very corner that, three years previously, Signor Gattica had built—for himself and for his wife—the beautifully flowered double-sized grave whose twin plots, side by side, had so struck the admiration of his great friend, Zorzi.

"Really a fine idea," Zorzi had said to his friend. "Resting side by side with your wife even after death. It looks like a double-bed lasting for ever."

And without delay—almost as if forestalling

his own end—he had ordered a similar grave to be built for his wife and himself.

A double-bed! Precisely! And in fact Signor Gattica—the most painstaking and methodical of all husbands—had laid his wife to rest on the right-hand plot of the grave so that, in his time, he might lie on her left, as he used to do in their double-bed at home.

Here lies
MARGHERITA GATTICA
An exemplary wife
Awaiting in peace
Her beloved husband.

he had written on his wife's grave.

The second slab was, of course, still bare, but the words had already been prepared by Signor Gattica, with a blank line for the day and the year of his death.

Here lies
ANTONIO GATTICA
Who rejoined his wife
On the . . .

"Pity," said Signor Gattica to himself, "that I cannot fill the last line! It would have looked so complete, so tidy, so symmetrical, with its proper date."

Little did he know then that only a few months later his dear friend Zorzi would die and his widow would entrust him with the choice of a suitable epitaph. Gattica had set to work at once; in fact he had promised the widow that he would select even better words than those he had used for his own wife. "Awaiting in peace her husband" was too cold, too plain, too stiff: let the words be altered for: "Here he lies awaiting for his faithful wife to rest at his side."

Wasn't this a thousand times better? Wouldn't his friend's widow appreciate the epitaph when visiting the grave? And how thankful she would be for the words he had so cleverly devised for his friend.

But to his amazement no word of thanks or praise came from the widow. Having knelt in a short prayer and having laid the bunch of flowers at the foot of the grave, she raised her long veil and—after a long perusal of the epitaph—she turned on him pale and frowning, her lips trembling and the big black wart on her chin twitching violently in sheer anger.

"Don't you like it?" he ventured timidly.

"Later! At home," came the answer like two pistol shots, "not here."

Again she turned to the grave, shook her head and bringing her black-edged handkerchief to her eyes she burst into violent sobs. Signor Gattica —in his turn—with two fingers pulled his scarlet handkerchief from his sleeve, removed his glasses and slowly wiped his eyes, first one and then the other.

"Not you! Not you!" shrieked the woman at him.

"W . . . Why?" he stammered.

"Later! At home!" the woman shot out again.

He looked at the epitaph, trying to find the cause of such violent anger. Was it perhaps the "faithful wife." But then isn't a wife always "faithful" just as a sky is always "blue?"

No, it wasn't that. What was worrying the widow's mind was not the "faithful wife" engraved on that slab, as Signor Gattica supposed. On the contrary she knew quite well that every cemetery was full of such lies, written for the vanity of the living more than for the glory of the dead. No, it wasn't the ridicule of her dead husband in claiming her as his "faithful wife."

What she minded was the offensive meaning of those words to her. Why had Signor Gattica written them? Why that "faithful wife" longing to rest at her husband's side, while he knew perfectly well that she had been his lover for three years while her husband was alive? Was he perhaps thinking that she—a respectable woman —would have continued to live with him as husband and wife without marrying, so that he might one day fill the empty grave by his wife's side? Did he really think that—for the mere sake of preserving these two epitaphs—she would accept to remain his mistress until he would rest by his "exemplary wife" and she would rejoin her late husband as his "faithful wife"?

No, never, never. For years she had lied: for years she had deceived her husband: that was a necessary lie, but now—after her husband's death—why lie again? Why deceive a dead husband merely because two twin graves had been too hastily prepared? Why that "faithful wife" which he wanted to force on her? Deceiving her husband while he was alive had been a necessity, but her honesty, her dignity, her pride could not allow her still to deceive a dead man: both Gattica and herself were now free, therefore either an honest and straightforward marriage or an immediate separation.

The discussion that ensued was long and heated. The widow's demand for an immediate marriage was spoiling all his plans. It was not merely a question of the two graves—which would have to be rebuilt all over again—but also a complete change in his widower's life to which he had already so comfortably settled down.

Why change? They had gone on for years while his friend Zorzi was alive and why should they change now that he was dead? Why marry when there was nobody to deceive any longer?

How could she talk of "settling their position" when the position had been settled long ago and nobody had the right to interfere with their lives? And what about the small revenue which she was receiving as long as her widowhood lasted? No, this marriage was merely an unreasonable and foolish idea to which he could never agree.

But the widow was adamant:

"Marriage or nothing."

And in vain—for eight months—he pleaded with her.

"No, no, marriage or nothing."

.   .   .   .   .

A WIDOW'S DILEMMA

At last—after eight months of heated arguments and pleadings—he told her that he would leave her and live by himself. It was a terrible shock for the widow. A week passed: then two, three, a month, without a word from him. The woman was frantic. Should she write to him? Should she call on him and tell him her distress? She was still puzzled as to what to do when a servant rushed from Signor Gattica begging her to go to him immediately as he was in great danger of his life.

Without hesitation she flew to his bedside torn by remorse. Forgetting her pride and everything else, for seven days and nights she sat by his bed trying to bring him back to life.

On the seventh day, when the doctors certified him out of danger, the widow—unable to restrain herself any longer—broke out into tears, thanking God for having brought him back to life. Her head bent on his bed, she could not help mentioning marriage again and Gattica—touched by her devotion—at last promised that as soon as he would recover he would arrange for the marriage to take place.

When he rose from bed, however, bent and trembling, he looked like the shadow of himself.

"I am finished, I am finished," he would warn her.

Yet a small improvement came during the summer and at last, feeling a little stronger, he urged her to get everything ready for their marriage.

"I will recover, I feel much better."

His home was still as Margherita—his wife—had left it on her death. Her bed alone had been removed into another room, nothing else. On the other hand the widow too had her own house, where nothing had been removed since her husband's death, not even the bed on which he had laid when dead. Where should they settle down? Which of the two homes was most suitable? Of course, thought the widow, she would sooner ask Gattica to give up his old house where the souvenir of Margherita was still so uncomfortably alive, but she did not feel like upsetting a sick man and it was decided that she would give up her own house and live in his. The furniture she would select from both houses, and the rest—including the four beds—would be sold by auction.

This, in fact, they did and they were married.

His health—almost as if the marriage had been

a good omen—improved during the first three months but at the beginning of the autumn he relapsed and he soon realized that all was finished for him.

From that day only one thought preyed on his mind, the thought of that little grave on the Pincetto. Where would his wife bury him? Would she still allow him to lie by his first wife, and fill up the missing line of the epitaph, or would she want to bury him in another grave—as her husband? Of course she had the right to do so, but then why had she forced him to marry her and thus break the symmetry of the whole thing? Why had she insisted on an unwanted marriage ceremony whose result was to upset the whole pre-arranged plan of the double grave for which everything was ready—including his own epitaph?

"Don't be silly," she would answer. "There is plenty of time to think about your grave."

But obstinate Gattica would not give way: "No, no, there is not much time left. Where will you bury me? I want to know it, I want to know it now."

He never knew it. He died suddenly, a few days later, grasping in his hand the sheet of paper on which he had prepared his own epitaph, with the empty space for the date.

"Nonsense," said his second wife—snatching the sheet from his lifeless hands. "Nonsense." Could he really think that she would bury him near his Margherita? Could he really think that she would let him rest next to another woman, merely for the sake of "symmetry"? Wasn't *she* his wife and then hadn't she a right to claim him for herself?

But then, where could she bury him? A new grave? Of course, but what about those two empty plots? The whole symmetry—so dear to him—would be upset.

She thought it over a whole night then the solution came to her in a flash. She would bury her second husband next to her first one. . . . They had been close and trusted friends all their lives: they will surely be pleased to rest next to each other for Eternity. As for herself she wouldn't mind, when the time would come, being set to rest next to Margherita, the "exemplary wife" who would thus no longer "be awaiting, in peace, her husband." After all, they had been good friends in lifetime, there was no reason why they too should not remain so even after death.

The decision was quickly carried out. When she saw Gattica's coffin at rest next to her first husband's grave she sighed with satisfaction. She carefully lit up the two little lamps at the bottom of each grave and gently laid two bunches of flowers, one on each grave.

Then—slowly moving to Margherita's grave—she put out the light which had been burning there since her death.

"No need for this light now," she thought. "It might spoil the symmetry and upset Gattica's peace."

Two husbands—two wives. She had no doubt that this was the most perfect solution of her dilemma. She felt quite sure that by doing as she had done she had interpreted Gattica's desire to its very word. "The symmetry"—she knew—was safe.

A MOTHER-IN-LAW

HONESTLY, the more I think of them and the less I am able to find out who of those two has lost his reason, Signor Ponza or his mother-in-law.

One of them must be mad—everyone in Valdana agrees on this point—but which of the two? It just happens that . . .

But let me first explain that although I am an entire stranger amongst the people of Valdana, I cannot but feel sympathy with them for their dismay since those two strange persons arrived in the quiet and usually happy little town. I sympathize with them because—although I am not concerned with the terrible blow which seems to have struck one of those two creatures to the point of making the other one lose his mind—I don't think it is fair to them to keep a whole town in suspense and anguish by so behaving that it is quite impossible to find out who says the truth and who is under the spell of some hallucination. Can you imagine us meeting them almost every day in the street (Valdana has only one main street where we all meet) knowing that one of the two is mad, watching them go, trying to scrutinize their faces and never being able to say for certain which of the two is insane? Perhaps —you may say to yourself—it's her—but then, immediately afterwards, you think it might be the reverse, so that if I had anything to do with the police I would order them both to quit the town.

But I am not the police and this is what has happened. Three months ago Signor Ponza, who holds a government post and has been sent from Rome, arrived at Valdana. He immediately rented a small flat on the fifth floor of "The Beehive," the large new building on the out-skirts of the town. A large balcony overlooks the fields, while three small windows open out on the yard. At one of these windows hangs a long, thin rope and a basket; by lowering the basket to the ground it is possible to bring up provisions and small parcels left by the traders, thus avoiding the long flight of stairs.

But Signor Ponza has also rented another flat —this time close to the centre of town—which he said, would be taken up by Signora Frola, his mother-in-law.

This has set the people of Valdana wondering: Why these two flats? If a mother cannot live apart from her married daughter, she usually goes and stays with her son-in-law, but if—as in the present case—she has found it imperative to follow her daughter to the same town and yet has decided to take a separate flat, it is quite obvious that there is something wrong in the family. "That man must be a brute," thought everyone at Valdana, and all the sympathies automatically swung in favour of the woman. Of course, they said, she may have her faults too, but would any decent man forbid his mother-in-law sharing his flat? Besides, Signor Ponza's appearances are all against him: short, rather thickly built, with an almost African dark complexion, wiry hair, thick eyebrows and a prominent threatening moustache, he is certainly not likely to win the immediate sympathies of those who meet him for the first time. On the contrary, the little middle-aged white-haired woman, frail and sad-looking, is the image of sweetness and kindness, and everybody feels quite sure that she must be terribly unhappy under the rule of such a man who even prevents her (as it has been found out) from calling at her daughter's flat.

Yet—to make matters even stranger—the old woman has never been heard to say a single word against her son-in-law; on the contrary, she seems grieved at the idea that anybody might think badly of him and is all eager to tell everyone what a good husband he is to his wife, what a devoted son he has proved to herself. . . . Yes, really a most devoted and exceptionally good-hearted son whose only fault—if fault may be—is perhaps an exaggerated love for his wife. But, she would add, after all, is there anything wrong in a man trying to have a wife all to himself and being jealous even of her mother? Jealousy? No, it wasn't the ordinary, common jealousy; it was a much different feeling, a feeling of intense love which could hardly be called a fault. Was it selfishness then? Of course not; can a man be called selfish who devotes himself entirely to a woman? No, he had merely built a close world round a woman, a world which he would not even allow her mother to force open. That is why she has resigned herself to live apart from her, although calling on her once a day and talking to her from the yard below.

"How are you to-day, Tildina?"

"Quite well, Mother, and you?"

"Excellent, darling. Now send down the basket."

And the little basket would come down carrying a note with the news of the day. That was their only meeting. For four years this had gone on, the old woman calling each day and each day carrying away the note sent her through the basket, wishing her daughter good-bye and again disappearing at the corner of the street, resigned and satisfied.

At Valdana, however, nobody could really believe the strange story. The ladies of the town (mainly the wives of her son-in-law's colleagues) had called on Signora Frola and had started gossiping, the gossip at last reaching Signor Ponza who, fearing the worst, decided that an "important confession" was due, to clear his position. He sent a word to the ladies whom he knew to be more friendly with his mother-in-law, asking them to receive him. Almost choked by emotion, his eyes deeper and gloomier than ever, grasping in his hand a white handkerchief with which to wipe his perspiration, he begged the ladies to keep a secret, a very important secret which he would have preferred to keep to himself but felt now forced to reveal. His mother-in-law, he said, was mad. Yes, she had become insane four years ago, when she heard of the death of her daughter. The shock was too great for her and from that day she refused to believe that her daughter had gone for ever, swearing that she was still alive. It had been impossible to convince her of the contrary and, out of charity for that distressed mother, he had thought it wiser to keep her illusion alive and to let her believe that his first wife was still alive. Yet, he added, it was not her daughter but his second wife who was living with him now and who too, out of sympathy for the poor woman, had agreed to appear at the window each day and to write the little note, locking herself in the flat for fear of being found out. "This," he concluded with tears in his eyes, "is the truth."

The good ladies of the town were staggered: several of them could hardly conceal their emotion and they all assured Signor Ponza of their sympathy for him, renewing their promise to keep the secret all to themselves. Somewhat reassured by their good words, Signor Ponza left the house, but no sooner had he gone than Signora Frola was announced.

She too had a secret to tell them, a very great secret. Of course they must swear to keep their lips sealed to everyone, or it might ruin the person who was dearest to her in the world, her excellent son-in-law. "It might ruin his whole career," she said gravely, "if it were known outside." And the secret was that Signor Ponza— the painstaking, sober, hard-working Government Official—was mad. He had become insane four years ago, when the idea had suddenly got into his brain that his wife was dead. The shock had been too great for him and from that day he was telling everyone that she had passed away and that her death had sent his mother-in-law insane. He is quite convinced, the poor fellow, that his wife has gone to a nursing home from which she has never come back," added the old lady with a sob, "and his mind has become so unhinged that, when she actually came back from the home, we had to stage another marriage with the help of relatives and friends, and make him believe that he was really marrying another woman. Recently," concluded Signora Frola, unable to hold back her emotion, "the tragedy has become even greater, for I believe he has recovered and he is fully aware that *his* wife is the same person as the first one, but—in his mad jealousy—he does not want anyone to approach her, not even her mother, and keeps her almost a recluse in the flat. Otherwise"—Signora Frola was quite convinced—"nobody could explain why he is so obliging and so taken with a mother-in-law who has ceased to be his wife's mother. And in the meantime, unfortunately," she sighs, "my daughter must allow everyone to believe that she is no longer herself, while in my turn I must allow everyone to believe that I am mad, merely because I say that my daughter is still alive. Can you understand, ladies, the terrible position of a mother who can only see her daughter through a window on the top floor of a building and let her son-in-law believe that he has married another woman? Yet I could find no other solution, and here I am, as you see me, accused of being insane for the sake of him who is really mad. Can you understand, ladies?"

Of course, the ladies could not understand, nor could anyone, nor can I, however much I have tried ever since, to solve this baffling problem. Why not ask the wife? you may ask. Yes, but can the wife be trusted when she swears that she is the second wife? Or is she, too, sheltering her husband's hallucination? Besides, how can anyone approach her when she refuses to open the door of the flat, saying that she is scared of meeting Signora Frola?

In the meantime Signor Ponza is equally convinced. "Sacrifice," he says, "sacrifice." Yes, but supposing he is really mad? Everyone in town would like to know how matters stand and when they see the two going along together, so friendly and so kind to each other, nobody would think that one of them is mad. Or are they perhaps both insane?

Often Signora Frola calls at the office of Signor Ponza and they go out shopping or for a walk together; they are on the best of terms; they seem perfectly pleased to be together and to exchange those courtesies which one expects only amongst people thoroughly in sympathy with each other; if she is tired, she gently leans on his arm and they both go along the street followed by hundreds of perplexed eyes who still wonder. . . . Who is really insane? Where is the truth and where is the shadow? Or is there more than one truth, perhaps? To answer this, one has first to answer: Who is mad, Signor Ponza or his mother-in-law? And so far the problem is still baffling the little provincial town of Valdana, usually so quiet and so happy.

WAR

THE passengers who had left Rome by the night express had had to stop until dawn at the small station of Fabriano in order to continue their journey by the small old-fashioned "local" joining the main line with Sulmona.

At dawn, in a stuffy and smoky second-class carriage in which five people had already spent the night, a bulky woman in deep mourning, was hoisted in—almost like a shapeless bundle. Behind her—puffing and moaning, followed her husband—a tiny man, thin and weakly, his face death-white, his eyes small and bright and looking shy and uneasy.

Having at last taken a seat he politely thanked the passengers who had helped his wife and who had made room for her; then he turned round to the woman trying to pull down the collar of her coat and politely enquired:

"Are you all right, dear?"

The wife, instead of answering, pulled up

her collar again to her eyes, so as to hide her
face.

"Nasty world," muttered the husband with a
sad smile.

And he felt it his duty to explain to his travelling companions that the poor woman was to be
pitied for the war was taking away from her her only
son, a boy of twenty to whom both had devoted
their entire life, even breaking up their home at
Sulmona to follow him to Rome where he had to
go as a student, then allowing him to volunteer
for war with an assurance, however, that at least
for six months he would not be sent to the front
and now, all of a sudden, receiving a wire saying
that he was due to leave in three days' time and
asking them to go and see him off.

The woman under the big coat was twisting
and wriggling, at times growling like a wild
animal, feeling certain that all those explanations
would not have aroused even a shadow of sympathy from those people who—most likely—were
in the same plight as herself. One of them, who
had been listening with particular attention,
said:

"You should thank God that your son is only
leaving now for the front. Mine has been sent

there the first day of the war. He has already come back twice wounded and been sent back again to the front."

"What about me? I have two sons and three nephews at the front," said another passenger.

"Maybe, but in our case it is our *only* son," ventured the husband.

"What difference can it make? You may spoil your only son with excessive attentions, but you cannot love him more than you would all your other children if you had any. Paternal love is not like bread that can be broken into pieces and spilt amongst the children in equal shares. A father gives *all* his love to each one of his children without discrimination, whether it be one or ten, and if I am suffering now for my two sons, I am not suffering half for each of them but double. . . ."

"True . . . true . . ." sighed the embarrassed husband, "but suppose (of course we all hope it will never be your case) a father has two sons at the front and he loses one of them, there is still one left to console him . . . while . . ."

"Yes," answered the other, getting cross, "a son left to console him but also a son left for whom he must survive, while in the case of the father of an only son if the son dies the father can die too and put an end to his distress. Which of the two positions is the worse? Don't you see how my case would be worse than yours?"

"Nonsense," interrupted another traveller, a fat, red-faced man with bloodshot eyes of the palest grey.

He was panting. From his bulging eyes seemed to spurt inner violence of an uncontrolled vitality which his weakened body could hardly contain.

"Nonsense," he repeated, trying to cover his mouth with his hand so as to hide the two missing front teeth. "Nonsense. Do we give life to our children for our own benefit?"

The other travellers stared at him in distress. The one who had had his son at the front since the first day of the war sighed: "You are right. Our children do not belong to us, they belong to the Country. . . ."

"Bosh," retorted the fat traveller. "Do we think of the Country when we give life to our children? Our sons are born because . . .well, because they must be born and when they come to life they take our own life with them. This is the truth. We belong to them but they never belong to us. And when they reach twenty they are exactly what we were at their age. We too had a father and mother, but there were so many other things as well . . . girls, cigarettes, illusions, new ties . . . and the Country, of course, whose call we would have answered—when we were twenty—even if father and mother had said no. Now, at our age, the love of our Country is still great, of course, but stronger than it is the love for our children. Is there any one of us here who wouldn't gladly take his son's place at the front if he could?"

There was a silence all round, everybody nodding as to approve.

"Why then," continued the fat man, "shouldn't we consider the feelings of our children when they are twenty? Isn't it natural that at their age they should consider the love for their Country (I am speaking of decent boys, of course) even greater than the love for us? Isn't it natural that it should be so, as after all they must look upon us as upon old boys who cannot move any more and must stay at home? If Country exists, if Country is a natural necessity like bread, of which each of us must eat in order not to die of hunger, somebody must go to defend it. And our sons go, when they are twenty, and they don't want tears, because if they die, they die inflamed and

happy (I am speaking, of course, of decent boys).
Now, if one dies young and happy, without
having the ugly sides of life, the boredom of it,
the pettiness, the bitterness of disillusion . . .
what more can we ask for him? Everyone should
stop crying: everyone should laugh, as I do . . .
or at least thank God—as I do—because my son,
before dying, sent me a message saying that he
was dying satisfied at having ended his life in the
best way he could have wished. That is why, as
you see, I do not even wear mourning. . . ."

He shook his light fawn coat as to show it; his
livid lip over his missing teeth was trembling,
his eyes were watery and motionless and soon
after he ended with a shrill laugh which might
well have been a sob.

"Quite so . . . quite so . . ." agreed the others.

The woman who, bundled in a corner under her
coat, had been sitting and listening had—for the
last three months—tried to find in the words of
her husband and her friends something to console
her in her deep sorrow, something that might
show her how a mother should resign herself to
send her son not even to death but to a probable
danger of life. Yet not a word had she found
amongst the many which had been said . . . and

her grief had been greater in seeing that nobody —as she thought—could share her feelings.

But now the words of the traveller amazed and almost stunned her. She suddenly realized that it wasn't the others who were wrong and could not understand her but herself who could not rise up to the same height of those fathers and mothers willing to resign themselves, without crying, not only to the departure of their sons but even to their death.

She lifted her head, she bent over from her corner trying to listen with great attention to the details which the fat man was giving to his companions about the way his son had fallen as a hero, for his King and his Country, happy and without regrets. It seemed to her that she had stumbled into a world she had never dreamt of, a world so far unknown to her and she was so pleased to hear everyone joining in congratulating that brave father who could so stoically speak of his child's death.

Then suddenly, just as if she had heard nothing of what had been said and almost as if waking up from a dream, she turned to the old man, asking him:

"Then . . . is your son really dead?"

Everybody stared at her. The old man, too, turned to look at her, fixing his great, bulging, horribly watery light grey eyes, deep in her face. For some little time he tried to answer, but words failed him. He looked and looked at her, almost as if only then—at that silly, incongruous question—he had suddenly realized at last that his son was really dead . . . gone for ever . . . for ever. His face contracted, became horribly distorted, then he snatched in haste a handkerchief from his pocket and, to the amazement of everyone, broke into harrowing, heart-rending, uncontrollable sobs.

SICILIAN TANGERINES

"Does Teresina live here?"

The butler, still in shirt sleeves but already in his starched collar, looked the young man up and down. With his rough coat collar turned up to his ears, and his hands blue and numb with cold, he stood at the top of the steps, boorishly facing the butler. He was carrying a dirty little bag in one hand, and in the other an old attaché case.

"Teresina? Who's that?" the servant asked in his turn, raising his thick eyebrows which looked like a pair of whiskers that had been shaven off his face and stuck there so as not to get lost.

The young man shook his head to let a dew-drop off the end of his nose, and then answered: "Teresina, the singer."

"Ho!" exclaimed the butler, with a satirical smile of surprise. "She's just called Teresina, is she? Good and plain? And who are you?"

"Is she in or not?" the young man asked,

with a frown and a snort. "Tell her that it's Micuccio and let me come in."

"But there's no one at home now," answered the servant, with the smile freezing on his lips. "Madame Sina Marnis is still at the theatre and . . ."

"And Aunt Martha?" Micuccio interrupted him.

"Oh, you are the nephew?" The servant immediately became all deferential. "No, sir, there's no one at home. The aunt is at the theatre too. I'm not expecting them back before one. It's the Gala Performance of your . . . let me see, what relation would Madam be to you, sir? Cousin then?"

Micuccio was a little troubled for a moment. "No . . . I'm not . . . not . . . her cousin really. I'm . . . I'm Micuccio Bonavino: she will know. I've come on purpose from the country."

After this answer the butler felt justified in dropping the "sir." He showed Micuccio into a dark little room next to the kitchen, whence there came loud snores. "Sit down here, and I will bring a light."

Micuccio looked in the direction of the snoring, but could discover nothing; he next looked into the kitchen, where a cook and a boy were preparing dinner. The smell of all the food overcame him; it made him feel sick and dizzy; he had eaten practically nothing since the morning, and he had travelled from the province of Messina, a whole night and day in the train.

The butler brought a light, and the person who was snoring in the room behind a curtain, which was hanging on a string from one wall to the other, grumbled sleepily: "Who is it?"

"Wake up, Dorina. Signor Bonvicino is here."

"Bonavino," Micuccio corrected him, as he blew on his fingers.

"Bonavino, a friend of Madam's. You do nothing but sleep. The bell rings and you never hear it. I can't do everything, mind you; I've got to lay, and to look after the cook who can't do a thing, as well as see to anyone who comes."

A loud yawn, keeping time with a good stretch, and finishing in a snort caused by a sudden shiver, was the answer to the butler's protest, and he went off grunting. "Oh, all right!"

Micuccio smiled and followed him with his eyes, across another room in semi-darkness, as far as a huge, brightly lit dining-room at the end, where a splendid table was spread. He was lost in admiration until once more the snoring made him turn and look at the curtain.

The butler, with his napkin under his arm, kept on passing in and out, and grumbling either at Dorina, who went on sleeping, or at the cook, who must have been new, engaged for that evening's celebrations, and worrying him by continually asking questions. Micuccio, so as not to worry him too, thought it wise to bottle up all the questions that *he* wanted to ask him. Also, he would have to tell him, or make him understand, that he was Teresina's fiancé, and he did not want to do that, though he did not know quite why, unless it was that the butler would then have to treat him, Micuccio, with deference. And Micuccio, seeing the butler so smart and self-possessed, although he still had no coat on, could not overcome the embarrassment he felt even at the mere thought. At one point, however, he could contain himself no longer, and asked, "Excuse me, but . . . this house . . . whose is it?"

"Ours, while we're here," the servant answered in a hurry. And Micuccio sat there shaking his head.

Good Heavens, it was true then! . . . Her fortune made! Big business! That butler, who looked like a fine gentleman, the cook and the boy, that Dorina snoring there, all were servants at the beck and call of Teresina. Whoever would have believed it?

He thought again of the miserable attic down in Messina, where Teresina used to live with her mother. Five years ago, in that far-away attic, if it had not been for him, mother and daughter would have died of hunger. And it had been he, he, who had discovered the fortune in Teresina's throat. In those days she would always be singing—like a house-sparrow, ignorant of her gift. She sang with defiance: she sang, so as not to think about her misery, her awful condition, which he did his best to alleviate in spite of the continual opposition of his parents at home—of his mother especially. How could he abandon Teresina in that state, after her father's death? Abandon her because she had nothing? He at least had a job, small though it was, as flautist in the municipal band.

Yes, it had been a real inspiration, prompted by heaven, taking advantage of her voice like that. It had been a lovely April day and Teresina was

humming a Sicilian tune by the attic window,
which framed a bright blue sky. Micuccio still
remembered the passionate words. Teresina had
been sad that day because of her father's recent
death, and because of the determined opposition
of his parents; and he too, he remembered was
sad—so much so that tears had come to his eyes
when he heard her sing. He had often heard her
sing the song before, but never like that. He had
been so struck that the next day, without warning
either her or her mother, he had brought the
conductor of his band, who was a friend of his,
back with him up into the attic. And so the first
singing lessons had begun, and for two years on
end he had spent almost all his wages on her. He
had hired a piano, bought the music, and even
given a friendly tip to the master. Good days
those! Teresina was longing to break away, and
launch herself into a future that promised her
much, so her master said: and in the meanwhile
such warm affection for him to show him how
grateful she felt! And what dreams of happiness
together!

But Aunt Martha, her mother, shook her head.
She had seen so much of this sort of thing before
in her life, poor old thing, she had no more faith

in the future: she feared for her daughter, and did not want her even to think of the possibility of escaping from the misery, to which they were now so much accustomed. And she knew too, how much the folly of their dangerous dream was costing him.

But they neither of them listened to her, and she had protested in vain when a young conductor-composer, who had heard Teresina at a concert, had declared that it was really a crime not to give her better teaching, and complete her musical training, by sending her to Naples. At all costs, she should go to the Conservatoire in Naples.

And then Micuccio, without thinking twice about it, had broken with his family, sold a small farm that a priest-uncle had left him, and sent Teresina to Naples to finish her training.

He had not seen her again since then. Letters there had been: he had had letters from her at the Conservatoire, and then, once Teresina was swept away in the full tide of her artistic life, and sought after by all the principal theatres, as the result of her astonishing success at Monte Carlo, letters had come from Aunt Martha. At the bottom of the shaky uncertain notes, that the poor old thing scrawled to him, there was always a word from her, from Teresina, who never had time to write herself. "Dear Micuccio, I confirm all Mother says. Keep well and love me." They had agreed that he was to leave her for five or six years to make her way without him: they were both young and could wait. And in the five years that had passed, he had always shown the letters to anyone who wanted to see them, so as to counteract the libellous things that his relations were spreading about Teresina and her mother. Then he had fallen ill, he was nearly dying: and it was at that point that Aunt Martha and Teresina, unknown to him, had sent a large sum of money to his address.

Some of it had gone during his illness, but the rest he had snatched bodily from his grasping relations, and now here he was to give it back to Teresina. He did not want the money, not a bit! Not because he resented it as charity, for he had already spent so much on her; and now in that house the money seemed to matter less than ever. He had waited so many years, he could wait still longer. Yet if Teresina had money to spare it was a sign that the future had opened out for her, and that the time was ripe for the old promise to be fulfilled, in spite of everyone who refused to believe it.

Micuccio got up, frowning as though to strengthen himself in this conclusion; he blew again on his icy hands and stamped his feet on the ground. "Cold?" the butler asked him as he passed. "They won't be long now. Come into the kitchen. It's more comfortable there."

Micuccio did not want to follow the butler's advice, for the butler disconcerted him with his grand airs. He sat down again and started thinking. He was worried. A little later a loud peal at the bell roused him.

"Dorina, there's Madam!" shrieked the butler, grabbing at his coat, to put it on as he ran to open the door; but he saw Micuccio starting to follow him, and stopped suddenly to tell him: "No, you stay here. Let me warn her first."

"O-o-oh!" wailed a sleepy voice from behind the curtain, and a huge fat woman with dyed hair appeared.

She waddled in, muffled in a shawl up to her eyes, and half-asleep. Micuccio stared at her, and she, with her eyes poking out of her head, looked at the stranger.

"It's Madam," Micuccio repeated. Dorina

suddenly came to. "Here I am," she said, pulling herself together and throwing her shawl behind the curtain. She directed her great body towards the front door.

The apparition of that painted harridan, and the butler's hints, put Micuccio into a sudden agony of foreboding. He heard the harsh voice of Aunt Martha: "Into the dining-room. Into the dining-room, Dorina." And the butler and Dorina went past him bearing magnificent baskets of flowers. He poked his head out to look at the brightly lit room at the end, and saw lots of men in tails, who were talking confusedly. His vision clouded. It was amazement as much as emotion, and he did not notice that his eyes had filled with tears. He shut them, and in the darkness drew himself taut, as if to resist the pain caused by a long pealing laugh. Was it Teresina's? O Lord, why was she laughing like that, in there?

A stifled cry made him open his eyes, and there before him he saw Aunt Martha, unrecognizable with her hat on, poor old thing, and weighed down by a rich velvet cloak. "What Micuccio, you here?"

"Aunt Martha . . ." he cried, almost frightened at seeing her.

"How's this?" pursued the old thing, quite upset. "No warning What's happened? When did you arrive? Only this evening? O dear. . . ."

"I came to . . ." stammered Micuccio, not knowing what to say.

"Wait a minute," Aunt Martha interrupted him. "What shall we do? You see what a lot of people have come, don't you, my dear? It's Teresina's celebration, her gala night. . . . Wait, wait in here a bit. . . ."

"If . . . if . . . you think I ought to go . . ." Micuccio tried to say, and his agony choked the words in his throat.

"No, wait here a bit," the good old thing hastened to answer, in great embarrassment.

"I . . . I wouldn't know where to go round here at this time of the day," Micuccio went on.

Aunt Martha left him, signing to him with her gloved hand to wait. She went into the dining-room, and to Micuccio a chasm seemed to open: there was suddenly silence. Then he heard, clearly and distinctly, Teresina's words: "One minute, gentlemen."

And once again his vision clouded, in the expectation of seeing her. But Teresina did not appear, and the conversation in the dining-

room started afresh. Instead, after a few minutes
which seemed to him an eternity, Aunt Martha
came back, without her hat this time, without her
cloak and gloves, and a little less embarrassed.
"Let's wait in here, shall we?" she said to him.
"I will stay with you. . . . They're having dinner
now. We will have supper together in here.
We'll talk over old times. . . . I can hardly
believe that we're together here, here all alone.
Such a lot of gentlemen in there. You do understand, don't you? Poor dear, she can't help it.
She's got to think of her career, you know. It's
got to be. You've seen the papers, haven't you?
Great goings on, my dear. But I . . . it's almost
too much for me . . . all the time. . . . I can
hardly believe that I'm here with you to-night."

And the little old woman, who had talked and
talked instinctively so as not to leave Micuccio
time to think, in the end smiled and rubbed her
hands as she looked at him affectionately.

Dorina came to lay the table, in a great hurry,
because dinner in the dining-room had already
begun.

"Will she come?" Micuccio asked darkly, in
a voice of agony. "I mean, shall I at least see her?"

"Of course she'll come," the old woman

answered quickly, overcoming her embarrassment with an effort. "As soon as she has a
moment to herself; she said so to me."

They looked at each other and smiled, as
though now at last they recognized each other.
With that smile through their awkwardness and
emotion their spirits had found a way to greet
each other. "You are Aunt Martha," Micuccio's
eyes spoke. "And you are my dear good Micuccio,
the same as ever, my poor boy," said Aunt
Martha's eyes. But the good woman dropped
hers at once so that Micuccio should not read
anything else in them. She rubbed her hands
again, and said, "Shall we have supper now?"

"I *am* hungry!" Micuccio exclaimed, happy
and reassured.

"Grace first. Here, in front of you, I can say
it," the old woman added with a mischievous look,
winking at him as she crossed herself.

The butler came in with the first course.
Micuccio watched carefully to see what Aunt
Martha did when she helped herself. But when
his turn came, on raising his hands, he remembered they were dirty from his long journey; he
blushed and felt embarrassed, and raised his eyes
to look at the butler, who, now all deferential,

bowed his head slightly and smiled, as though inviting him to help himself. Fortunately Aunt Martha came to the rescue. "Here, Micuccio, I'll serve you."

He could have kissed her in his gratitude.

As soon as he was served and the butler out of the room, he too hastily crossed himself. "Good boy!" Aunt Martha said encouragingly.

And he felt quite happy and at his ease, and set about his supper as though he'd never seen food in his life before, without another thought of his hands or of the butler. And yet every time the butler, going in and out of the dining-room, opened the glass door and let out a wave of confused words or bursts of laughter, he would turn and his troubled gaze would then meet the sad, affectionate eyes of the old woman, as though he expected to find the answer there. But, instead, in them he read a supplication to ask nothing for the present, to put off explanations till later. And they would both smile and start eating again, and talk of their distant country and of their friends and acquaintances, of whom Aunt Martha required endless news.

"Aren't you having anything to drink?"

Micuccio stretched out to take the bottle, but

at that instant, the dining-room door opened again: a rustle of silk, quick steps, a movement and a flash, as though the little room had been suddenly lit up to blind him.

"Teresina. . . ."

And his voice died on his lips in amazement. What a vision!

With his face burning, his eyes ablaze, and his mouth wide open, he stared at her, dazed. How could it be her, like that! Her breast, her shoulders and her arms were bare . . . all sparkling with satin and jewels. He no longer saw her as a real, live person before him. . . . What was she saying to him? Neither her voice, nor her eyes, nor her smile, nothing did he recognize of her in that dream vision. "How are you getting on? You're well now, aren't you Micuccio? Well done! You have been ill, you told me. We'll see each other again soon. . . . Meanwhile you've got Mother with you. That's all right, isn't it?"

And Teresina rushed back into the dining-room.

"Won't you eat any more?" Aunt Martha asked him tentatively, so as to break the silence of his stupefaction. He barely turned to look at her.

"Eat," insisted the old woman, pointing at his plate.

Micuccio put two fingers up to his dirty, crumpled collar, and stretched at it, trying to draw a deep breath. . . . "Eat?"

And he shook his fingers several times near his chin, as if to say, "I can't manage any more. I really can't." He went on sitting there in silence, degraded, lost in the vision of some minutes before; and then murmured: "What has she turned into? . . ."

And he saw that Aunt Martha was shaking her head bitterly, and that she also had stopped eating, as though she were waiting.

"But it's absolutely impossible now . . ." he added, almost to himself, with his eyes shut.

In the darkness he now saw the chasm that had opened between them. No, that wasn't his Teresina, not that person. It was all over—ages ago. Ages ago, and he, like a fool, had only seen it now. . . . They had told him so at home, and he had refused to believe it. . . . And now, what a fool he was making of himself there, in that house. If all those men, and that butler even, had known that he, Micuccio Bonavino, had strained every nerve to come from so far, thirty-six hours by train, believing quite seriously that he was still the fiancé of that vision of beauty, what guffaws there would be from those men, and that butler and the cook and the boy and Dorina! What guffaws if Teresina had dragged him into their presence, there in the dining-room, and said, "Look, this poor little man, this flute-player, says that he wants to become my husband." She herself had promised, it was true; but how could he then have imagined that one day she would turn into this? And it was also true that it was he who had made this possible for her, and had provided her with the means of getting there; but she had now gone so far, so very far, that he, left behind, the same as ever, to play the flute on Sundays in the local square, how could he ever reach her? Absolutely out of the question. And what were those few poor coins spent on her, now that she had become such a grand lady! He felt ashamed even to think that anyone could have suspected that he, by coming, was wanting to make some claim, on the strength of those few wretched coins. He remembered in that instant that he had the money in his pocket that Teresina had sent him during his illness. He blushed and felt ashamed. He put one hand into his breast

pocket, where he kept his portfolio, and said
quickly, "I came, Aunt Martha, also to give you
back this money that you sent me. What was it
supposed to be? Payment? Repayment? I see
that Teresina has now become a . . . a . . . star. I
see that . . . nothing! It's quite impossible! But
this money, no, I did not deserve that from her.
It's all over, and we won't say anything more
about it . . . but no money, no I'm sorry only that
it's not all here."

"What are you saying, my boy?" Aunt
Martha tried to interrupt him with tears in her
eyes. Micuccio signed to her to be quiet.

"I did not spend it. It was my relations, during
my illness, and I knew nothing about it. But that
can make up for the little bit that I spent on
her, you remember? Don't let's bother about it
any more. . . . Here's what's left, and I'm going."

"What? So quickly?" Aunt Martha cried,
trying to keep him back. "Do wait anyhow and
tell Teresina. Didn't you hear how she wanted
to see you again? I will go and tell her."

"No, it's no good," Micuccio answered firmly.
"Leave her there with those men. She's in the
right place there. I, poor wretch . . . I've seen
her; that's enough for me. . . . Oh, well, go

if you like, you go in there to.... listen to how they're laughing.... I don't want them to laugh at me. I'm going."

Aunt Martha interpreted this sudden resolution of Micuccio's in the worst sense, as a gesture of scorn, an act of jealousy. It now seemed to her, poor thing, that anyone seeing her daughter would immediately believe the worst of her. It was for this reason that she wept inconsolably, ceaselessly bearing her affliction through that life of hateful luxury, which was making her tired old age indecent and dishonourable.

"But I can no longer protect her, my son," she let out.

"Why?" Micuccio asked; and he read suddenly in her eyes the suspicion that had not struck him till then. His face grew dark.

The little old woman was lost in her misery. She hid her face in her quivering hands, but could not stem the onslaught of her tears.

"Yes, go away, my son, go away," she said amid stifling sobs. "She is not for you any longer, you are quite right. If only you had listened to me!"

"Then," Micuccio broke in, bending over her and forcibly pulling one hand from her face.

But with such anguish and misery did she look at him and beg his mercy, putting one of her fingers up to her mouth, that he restrained himself, and added in another voice, forcing himself to speak softly, "Well, then, you . . . you are no more worthy than I am. But it's enough; I'm going all the same—or rather, all the more reason now. . . . What a fool I am, Aunt Martha. I had not understood. Don't cry. Anyhow, what's the good? Money, they say, money. . . ."

He took his little attaché case and bag from under the table, and was starting to go, when he remembered that in the bag were some fine tangerines that he had brought for Teresina from the country.

"Look, Aunt Martha," he began. He opened the bag and tipped the fresh sweet-smelling fruit on to the table. "What if I threw all these tangerines at those men in there?" he added.

"No, for Heaven's sake," groaned the poor old thing amid her sobs, begging him once more to be quiet.

"No, all right, I won't," Micuccio answered, laughing a bitter laugh, and putting the empty bag into his pocket. "I brought them for her, but I'm leaving them all now for you, Aunt

Martha." He took one and held it up to her nose. "Smell, Aunt Martha, smell the good scent of our country. And to think that I have even paid the local customs duty on them. Enough. For you only, remember. And to her say 'Good luck' in my name."

He picked up his attaché case and went out. But on the stairs a feeling of agonizing fear overwhelmed him. He was alone and abandoned at night in a great unknown city, far from his own country. He was disillusioned, degraded, scorned. He reached the main door and saw that it was pouring with rain. He had not the courage to venture forth into the unknown streets in that downpour. He went in again very quietly, climbed one flight of stairs and sat down on the top step. Resting his elbows on his knees and his head in his hands, he began crying silently.

When dinner was over, Sina Marnis came once again into the little room. She found her mother crying too, all alone, while in there those men were joking and laughing. "Has he gone?" she asked in surprise. Aunt Martha nodded without looking at her. Sina stared into vacancy and gave a deep sigh. "Poor thing. . . ." But she soon had to smile.

"Look," her mother said to her, no longer checking her tears. "He brought you these tangerines."

"Oh, how lovely!" cried Sina, jumping up. She put out her hand and took as many as she could carry.

"No, not in there!" her mother protested with feeling. But Sina shrugged her shoulders, and ran into the dining-room shouting: "Look, Sicilian tangerines!"

PROFESSOR LAMIS' VENGEANCE

BERNARDINO LAMIS, Professor of Ecclesiastical History, half closed his eyes, and as was his habit upon all grave occasions, cupped his stone-bald head in his frail, trembling hands, tipped with tiny nails, resembling shining, pink shells, and addressing himself to the only two students who followed his lectures with tenacious faithfulness, he said:

"Gentlemen, at our next lecture we shall discuss the Albigensian Heresy."

One of the two students, Ciotta, a bronzed whale of a youth, ground his teeth and rubbed his hands energetically. The other, however, pale Vanicoli, with blond, straight hair, and wearing a doomed expression, pouted, and his pale, languishing eyes looked more mournful than ever. He sniffed the air as if scenting some disagreeable odour, a sign indicating that in view of the private discussions he had had with his venerable master, he realized what painful efforts the development of this theme would cost him. In fact Vanicoli knew that about six months before, there had appeared in Germany (at Halle-on-S) a colossal monograph on the Albigensian Heresy by H. von Grobler, which the critics had lauded to the skies. Three years before that, Bernardino Lamis had written two considerable tomes on the same subject, of which Grobler had not taken the least notice, except for a brief reference of adverse comment.

This was a direct blow at Bernardino Lamis' heart. He was even more hurt and indignant by the Italian critics, who, with eyes sealed, had also sung the praises of the German work, without even referring to his two earlier volumes, and without wasting a word on refuting the indignities with which the German scribe had affronted their national writer.

Thus Bernardino Lamis, as they were leaving the University, had every reason to yield to bitterness before these two faithful young men, who usually accompanied him to his front door.

He talked to them about the blatant charlatanry which, from political fields, had dared to trespass into the pastures of literature. But now, alas! it had even penetrated into the sacred and inviolable precincts of science. He talked about the vulgar servility, deep-rooted in the Italian character, of a people who think that anything from other lands or across the seas is bound to be a precious gem, while anything produced in Italy must be paste. By way of winding up, he made allusion to the irrefutable arguments he would muster against his adversary in his forthcoming lecture. Ciotta, anticipating the professor's ironic, liverish verve, again rubbed his hands, while Vanicoli, thoroughly saddened, heaved a sigh.

A few moments later, Pr. Lamis became silent and assumed an absent-minded air—a hint to his two pupils that he wished to be left alone.

After each of these walks, he made a little detour for the sake of relaxation. Before making for Governo-Vecchio Street, where he lived, he was in the habit of visiting (furtively, as he thought) a confectioner's shop, from which he always emerged within a few minutes carrying a paper bag.

His two pupils knew that he had not enough to feed a bird with, and consequently they could not understand the mystifying acquisition of a bagful of confectionery two or three times a week.

One day, urged by curiosity, Ciotta could not resist entering the shop and to enquire what the professor bought.

"Macaroons, meringues and madeleines."

Who could that be for?

Vanicoli suggested that it was for his little nephews and nieces but Ciotta said that he would unhesitatingly risk his right hand that the professor consumed the delicacies himself.

Not only this little weakness for delicacies, but many other things, too, might have been forgiven this man who, for the love of knowledge, had reduced himself to nothing. His vaulted shoulders looked as if they had slipped and were only held painfully in position by the long protruding neck, as if under a yoke. Between the hat and the nape of the neck the professor's baldness was apparent in the dim moonlight. A thin fringe of white hair trembled on the nape and passing behind the ears formed a collar-like beard on cheeks and chin.

Of course, neither Ciotta nor Vanicoli could possibly have known that Bernardino Lamis carried home his daily meal in that paper bag.

Two years previously, the family of one of his brothers, who had died suddenly, had fallen on his shoulders: a sister-in-law, one of hell's own furies, with seven children, the eldest of whom was barely eleven years old. It should be mentioned that Professor Lamis himself had never married, because he did not want to be distracted from his studies.

He did not even afford himself a housekeeper, for fear that there might be ructions with his sister-in-law, and in any case, he had no need of one. Nor had he troubled to bring his bed along; he slept in his large arm-chair, with a shawl thrown over his shoulders and wrapped up in a woollen rug. He did no cooking. Following Fletcher's theory, he ate very little and masticated well. He emptied the famous paper bags into his ample trouser pockets, half into the right, and half into the left, and while he wrote or worked, standing up as was his wont, he munched either a macaroon, a meringue or a madeleine. If he was thirsty, he drank water. After that year in hell, he now felt himself in paradise.

And just then that putrid von Grobler must come and spoil his happiness with his outrageous book on the Albigensian Heresy.

On that same day, the moment he had reached home, Bernardino Lamis set to work feverishly.

He had only two days in which to prepare that lecture which lay so near to his heart. He wanted it to be formidable; each word was to be a pointed shaft against that Teuton, von Grobler.

He was in the habit of drawing up his lectures in a diminutive calligraphy on foolscap paper, from the first word to the last. Afterwards, at the University, he would read it out, in a slow, grave voice, with head thrown back and puckered forehead, contracting his eyebrows to enable him to peer through his eye-glasses which were riding astride his nose. His two disciples had ample time to take down what he said, as if by dictation.

Lamis never took the chair; he preferred to sit humbly at the small table beneath it. The benches were arranged in four rows, amphitheatre-fashion. As the room was very dark, Ciotta and Vanicoli usually occupied seats in the last row, one on the extreme left, the other on the extreme right, so as to get a little illumination from the grilled skylights above. The professor could only hear the scratching of their pens.

There, in that lecture hall, since nobody had stood up to defend him, and the Press had refused him even a tiny space wherein to defend himself, after thirty years of lecturing at the University and numerous strictly scientific publications, there, in that very lecture hall, he would revenge himself on that German by delivering a memorable lecture.

Before starting he decided to read his critical notes on von Grobler's book. He took them from a drawer in his desk and blew the dust off the paper. While writing he allowed himself to be tempted to incorporate the whole of his notes in his lecture, deciding there was nothing super-fluous in them, not even a full stop or a comma. How could he resist those expressions, so subtle, spontaneous, and efficacious? How could he resist those decisive arguments and others, even more convincing, that came to him as he wrote?

On the morning of the day when Bernardino Lamis was to deliver his lecture he found on his desk more than fifteen pages, instead of six, closely covered in his tiny handwriting.

He felt distressed.

Most scrupulous in all his professional duties, at the beginning of each year he always drew up a schedule of the subjects he would be discussing in his lectures and to this schedule he adhered rigorously. Because of that confounded publica-tion of von Grobler's book, he had already made a concession to his self-esteem by including this year, so to speak without any reason, a lecture on the Albigensian Heresy. Under the circumstances it was, therefore, quite impossible to devote more than one lecture to it. On no account would he have it said that out of anger or in a spirit of vengeance Professor Lamis had, outside of the curriculum, and at greater length than was absolutely necessary lectured on a subject not entered in the annual agenda.

Consequently it was imperative, in the few remaining hours, to reduce the fifteen pages he had written to eight or nine at the most. To make these cuts cost him such mental effort that he never noticed the hailstones, the lightning and the clattering noise of the storm which had suddenly overtaken Rome. When he arrived at the front door, a long roll of paper tucked under his arm, it was raining in torrents. What should he do? He mounted the stairs again to arm himself with an umbrella, and in blinding rain he started on his way, sheltering his "formidable" lecture as best he could.

He arrived at the university in a pitiable condition—soaked to the skin. He left his umbrella in the hall porter's lodge, shook the rain off his back by stamping and ascended the stairs still wiping his face.

The classroom, a sombre apartment even on a bright day, looked like a catacomb under that infernal sky. It was hardly possible to see. All the same on entering the room, Professor Lamis, who habitually never raised his head, had the consolation of perceiving in outline a well-dressed auditorium. In his heart he felt grateful to his two disciples. They had obviously informed their colleagues of the particular care and trouble the old professor had taken over a lecture which had cost him so much effort, which would reveal a treasure-trove of knowledge and which would be pierced with finely pointed shafts of irony.

Overcome by his emotions, he put down his hat, and contrary to all precedent, he took the chair. On that day his frail hands trembled so that he could hardly set his pince-nez on the tip of his nose. Complete silence reigned in the classroom. Having unrolled his papers, Professor Lamis began to read with a voice so powerful and vibrant that he was amazed at himself. Ah, to what heights he would soar when he came to tackling the polemics after these preliminary exhortations, for which this undertone was quite good enough. But already the professor was no longer master of himself. As if he had been bitten by the viperous shafts of his own style, he felt occasional tremors running all over his body. Louder and louder he raised his voice, gesticulating with his arms. On this particular day, Professor Lamis, usually so severe and restrained, actually gesticulated! He had accumulated too much bile in the last six months. The servility and the silence of the Italian Press had filled him with immense indignation.

The moment of his revenge had arrived. All these brave young men who were listening to him fervently would talk of this memorable lecture. They would tell how on that particular day the professor had actually taken the chair so that his withering retort from the collegium of Rome should smite not only von Grobler, but the whole of Germany.

For about three-quarters of an hour he had read thus, growing more and more heated and vibrant, when his pupil Ciotta, who had been overtaken by an even worse downpour and had taken shelter in a porch furtively entered the room. He had hoped that the professor would not have ventured forth in this kind of weather to deliver his lecture.

PROFESSOR LAMIS' VENGEANCE

Downstairs the hall porter had handed him a note from Vanicoli asking him to explain his absence to their very dear master. As he was about to leave the house the previous evening, he had made a false step and had fallen downstairs, dislocating his arm; to his deep regret, he was therefore, unable to attend the lecture.

But who was Professor Lamis addressing with such fervour? Ciotta entered the classroom very quietly, on tip-toe, and looked around. In spite of the dim light, he, too, saw the amphitheatre filled with students and was amazed at the sight.

On that particular day about twenty motionless figures, sprawling in all sorts of listening attitudes, formed Professor Lamis' audience in the sombre classroom.

Ciotta looked at them terrified. His blood jelled at the sight of his master delivering his lecture with so much ardour to all these overcoats. Ciotta became frightened and withdrew.

At that moment a band of students, probably owners of the immobile overcoats, surged noisily from a lecture-room on the right.

"For the love of Mike, don't go in there! Professor Lamis is in the room."

"What is he doing?" asked the young men, puzzled by Ciotta's haggard look.

The latter put a finger to his lips and, his eyes distended, said in a low voice:

"He is talking to himself."

They went off, bursting into irrepressible laughter.

Ciotta quickly closed the classroom door and called imploringly:

"Silence, for the love of Mike, silence! Don't inflict this mortification on that poor old soul. He is delivering his lecture on the Albigensian Heresy."

The students, promising not to make any noise, wanted to open the door very gently in order to enjoy the spectacle of their overcoats listening motionless to the formidable lecture of Professor Lamis in the shadowy classroom.

"But manicheism, gentlemen, manicheism, what is that really? Ask yourselves. If the first Albigensians, according to the illustrious German historian, Hans von Grobler. . . ."

HIS MEDALS

ALL that morning, Sciarame' had been pacing his little room like a lion in a cage.

On more than one occasion Roro', his step-daughter, had peeped through the door to ask him:

"What are you looking for?"

Whereupon Sciarame', trying to hide his worry, had answered at first that he was searching for his stick.

"But there it is, can't you see it? There, in that corner."

And Roro' had handed it to him. Then, a little later, he had asked for a handkerchief. Roro' had given him a clean one, but still Sciarame' would not leave the room.

The truth was that Sciarame' was summoning up his courage to speak to his step-daughter about something very important but, so far, he had failed. He had failed because he was as shy of her as he had always been of his wife, now dead for the last seven years, dead "from a broken heart"—Roro' used to say—"due to her husband's stupidity."

A succession of bad years had forced Sciarame'—at one time comfortably off—to sell first his small lemon and orange orchards and then the house, so that, at sixty-eight years of age, he had been compelled to turn a middleman, selling on commission those very oranges and lemons which were once his own.

Poor Sciarame'! He who had always looked upon middlemen as thieves was now finding himself one of them; tramping from morning to night at his age, weak and ailing, dragging his swollen feet buried in a pair of ragged felt shoes, fighting for a small commission which dealers would throw at him more as a charity than as a due.

Those who had known him before felt sorry for him. Yet everyone was certain that all these trials were more than made up for on national holidays when—dressed up in a faded red shirt, with the large handkerchief tied round his neck and the pointed hat well over his eyes—he would join the Garibaldian veterans in their procession, with his fine row of medals shining on his breast.

Seven medals!

And yet, when walking with his old companions behind the Garibaldian flag, he looked almost like a lost dog. He would constantly lift his left arm tugging at his beard or stroking his moustache, as though shy and anxious to hide those very medals of which he was so proud.

Many of his friends, seeing him pass by, would shout:

"Long live the Fatherland, Sciarame'! Long live Italy!"

Shy and smiling, he would lower his bald little eyes, answering in a low voice:

"Long live Italy! Hurrah! Hurrah!"

. . . . .

The headquarters of the Garibaldian Veterans' Society occupied a ground-floor room of the last shanty left in Sciarame's possession. A steep wooden staircase led to two rooms upstairs, one for his step-daughter and one for himself. On the front door, half covered by a stray branch of jasmine gracefully stretching from Roro's window, was a large inscription in bold red lettering: "GARIBALDIAN VETERANS' SOCIETY."

The room was scantily furnished: a large table, covered with a green cloth, specially reserved for the Council; a smaller table for the display of newspapers and magazines; an old and dusty bookcase stuffed with volumes mostly uncut. On the walls hung a life-size colour-print of Garibaldi; a portrait of Mazzini—of smaller size; a portrait of Carlo Cattaneo—still smaller; and—surrounded by ribbons, paper lanterns and flags—a print commemorating the "Death of the Hero of the Two Worlds."

Every morning Roro', having tidied up the two rooms upstairs, would put on her famous flaming red blouse and would go down to the ground-floor room where, sitting by the door, she would talk to her neighbours while carrying on with her sewing. She was a beautiful girl, dark and healthy, and they called her "La Garibaldina."

It so happened that, that very day, Sciarame' had to ask his step-daughter not to come down to that room any more and to remain upstairs instead. For Amilcare Bellone, the President of the Association, had complained to him, not because of this habit of Roro's who, after all, was mistress in her own home, but because of a certain young fellow, Rosalino La Rosa, who—with the excuse of coming to read the papers—would go there every morning and pretend to be a Garibaldian veteran when, in fact, he had merely fought in Greece against the Turks.

This La Rosa, rich and lazy, was so proud of his youthful adventure that it had almost become an obsession with him and he could speak of nothing else. One of the three companions who had fought with him—Gasperi—had been slightly wounded at Domokos and Rosalino spoke of this almost as though the wound had been his own. Tall, slender, with a long square-cut, reddish beard and a generous turned-up moustache which, if properly stretched, could easily have been tied into a knot at the back of his neck, Rosalino La Rosa was certainly a handsome young fellow.

It was not difficult to realize that his visits to the headquarters were not so much for the purpose of reading the papers as for the double purpose of letting everyone know that he was quite at home with the Garibaldians and of taking the opportunity for a little flirtation with Roro', the girl with the red blouse.

Sciarame' had noticed it too, but he also knew that Roro' was a level-headed girl and that the young man was comfortably off. Could he, in all consciousness, rule out the possibility of a profitable wedding for his step-daughter? He was old and poor; what would happen to the girl if he died and she had not found a husband? Besides, he wasn't her real father and hadn't sufficient authority to forbid her a thing which he not only considered harmless but eventually profitable to her.

On the other hand, he could not say that the President was altogether wrong. These were family matters which it was wiser to keep away from the Veterans' Society. Neighbours were already gossiping, some of them speaking of an intrigue between La Rosa and Roro' under the shadow of the Society and which the President— rightly jealous of the Society's good name—could not allow. What was Sciarame' to do? How should he approach Roro' on the subject?

The poor old man had been puzzling himself for over an hour, when Roro' herself gave him the lead.

Wearing her flaming red blouse, she bounced into her step-father's room:

"Still here? Are you or are you not going out this morning? I haven't even had an opportunity of tidying your room. I'm going downstairs."

"Wait . . . Roro' . . . listen," started Sciarame',

mustering up his courage. "That's just what I wanted to tell you."

"What?"

"That you . . . well, you see . . . I mean, couldn't you . . . wouldn't you prefer to work here, upstairs in your room, rather than downstairs?"

"And may I ask why?"

"Well . . . well, you see, because . . . because downstairs, you see, the members . . ."

Roro' raised her eyebrows in surprise.

"A new idea is it? Have the honourable gentlemen decided to pay you for the rent of the room, then?"

Sciarame' grinned, as though amused by Roro's remark.

"Of course," he said, "it's true that they don't . . . they don't pay for the room."

"Then what do they want?" asked Roro' haughtily. "Are they going to dictate terms in our house?"

"No! that has nothing to do with it!" Sciarame' tried to explain. "It was my own offer. . . ."

"Yes, but for the evenings only," agreed Roro'. "They are free to do as they like in the evenings, since you had the bright idea of offering them a free shelter, here. I alone know how difficult it is for me to get to sleep with all that talking, shouting and mad singing going on downstairs! Now, on top of all this, they would want me . . ."

"It isn't you," Sciarame' interrupted, "not really you, my dear. . . ."

"I see!" said Roro' becoming serious. "I knew what you meant even before you began to speak. You can tell the honourable gentlemen to mind their own business and to let me look after my own; and if this doesn't suit them let them find another place and I shall not be sorry. In my house I meet whom I like. I have to ask nobody's permission but yours. Now tell me: have you by any chance lost trust in me?"

"Of course not, my dear! Of course not!"

"Then that's enough! I have nothing further to tell you."

And Roro', her face as red as her blouse, turned her shoulders on him and went downstairs, fuming with rage.

Sciarame' gulped, then, standing in the centre of the room, he rubbed his lips, worried and angry with himself, with Roro' and with the veterans. Something he must do, but what?

Better go out, perhaps. Some fresh air! In the open, who knows, some bright idea might occur to him.

Hobbling carefully down the stairs, one hand leaning on the wall and the other on the stick, dragging down one swollen foot after another and panting at each step, he crossed the ground-floor room, leaving the house without a word. Roro'—sitting at her usual place—was too fully absorbed in conversation with one of the neighbours to take any notice of him.

. . . . .

Oh, what a relief it would have been for him if that blessed child were married! A marriage with La Rosa was—all things considered—unlikely: first of all because Roro' was poor, and then because she was known as "La Garibaldina," while La Rosa's family wanted—for their light-headed son—a steady, sensible young woman, without patriotic vagaries. Not that Roro' had ever had any such vagaries, but having got the name for them she was perhaps using it now, like a spider with his web, to entangle that young butterfly—La Rosa.

"After all, why not?" sighed Sciarame', thinking how entangled the butterfly seemed already to be.

In all fairness, how could he destroy that cobweb just now, merely to satisfy the honourable veterans who did not even pay any rent? And, after all, what was the President's grievance? He had complained that, in Greece, La Rosa had worn a red shirt. Silly jealousy! The red shirt on that young man's back was a sacrilege to the President's eyes: making him as wild as a bull. If it had been any other young man he could have gone to the Society to read the papers and Bellone would have taken no notice of him, but La Rosa. . . .

Deeply absorbed with his thoughts, Sciarame' reached the main square of the village and seated himself, as he did each day, at one of the small tables outside the café.

There he would stop for hours, waiting for someone to find him an odd job, and eventually falling asleep from boredom, never ordering anything, not even a glass of water with a taste of kummel. Yet the proprietor welcomed him, knowing that clients liked to hear his tales of Garibaldi and of his battles. Sciarame' would speak of them with touching sadness, shaking his

head and half closing his bald little eyes. He
would describe painful episodes, the dead, the
wounded, without a trace of boasting, so that—in
the end—those who had expected to be amused
by his talk became gloomy and distressed at this
little old man whose poverty and misery seemed
to have killed even the enthusiasm and the fire of
the past.

That morning one of the customers, seeing him
more depressed than ever, had tried to cheer him
up:

"Don't worry, Sciarame'! The King's birthday will soon be here: a fine chance for an airing
to the old red shirt!"

Sciarame', without moving from his seat, had
made a quick gesture with his hands as if to say
that far different thoughts were in his head. He
was about to rest his chin on the knob of his
stick when he heard the President yelling his
name from across the piazza: "Sciarame',
Sciarame'!" Sciarame' jumped to his feet to inform him:

"I have told her. . . . I have told her all
right!"

But Bellone, seizing him by the arm and
advancing a fist under his nose shouted:

"Liar! He is there again!"

"Who?"

"La Rosa."

"There?"

"Yes, and now I'll show you what I'll do with him. I'll kick him out myself."

"For heaven's sake!" begged Sciarame', "don't start a row. Let *me* go. I promise that he will never set his foot in there again. I thought Roro' would tell him. . . . But leave it to me. . . ."

The President jeered at him; then, without releasing his grip, he asked:

"Shall I tell you what you are?"

Sciarame' smiled bitterly, shrugging his shoulders.

"A blockhead?" he said. "I know it, but did you only find it out now?"

And off he went, stooping, shaking his head, leaning heavily on his stick.

.   .   .   .   .

When Roro'—sitting by the door—saw him approaching, she made a hasty sign for La Rosa to move away and to sit at the table covered with newspapers. In a stride La Rosa was there, at

PUBLIC LIBRARY,
RAWTENSTALL.

once opening a magazine and engrossed in reading it.

"Back so soon?" she asked her step-father, trying to look indifferent. "What's wrong?"

Sciarame' glanced first at La Rosa who, his elbows on the table and his head sunk between his hands, was pretending to read, and then turned to his step-daughter:

"I had asked you to stop upstairs."

"And I had told you that in my house . . ." began Roro'. But Sciarame' cut her short, raising his stick and pointing to the staircase:

"Go upstairs and don't argue! I have a few words to say to Signor La Rosa."

"To me?" said the young man, as though falling from the clouds and pulling at his fine moustache. "To me?" he repeated.

He rose to his feet, and, moving close to Sciarame', stretched himself to his full height, making him look smaller than ever.

"Yes, to you," he stammered, "but pray, be seated. . . . All I wanted to tell you was. . . . You can go, Roro'; leave us alone, please."

Rosalino La Rosa bent himself in two to bid Roro' good-bye, and when she had gone Sciarame' —turning to him with a smile—began:

"I know you are a good fellow, my dear Don Rosalino. . . ."

"My deepest thanks!"

"No, it is true," resumed Sciarame', "and I, for one, feel honoured. . . ."

"My deepest thanks!"

"No, no, it is true, I tell you. I am deeply honoured, my dear Don Rosalino, that you should come here to . . . to read the papers. But, well, how can I explain? I am the master here and yet I am not the master. You see: these are the Head-quarters of the Society of Veterans and I have certain responsibilities towards my fellow members. . . . Perhaps you don't understand. . . ."

"No, I don't," said La Rosa abruptly.

"Well," continued Sciarame', "I will put it in another way; you are a good fellow who comes here to read the papers; as far as I am concerned you are welcome, but these papers . . . well, these papers, unfortunately, do not belong to me. . . . If they were mine. . . . Why, you could have them all, of course! But as you are not a member. . . ."

"Stop," shouted La Rosa, furious and raising his hand. "Stop. I knew you would say this; I was waiting for it. I am not a member, am I?

And now answer this: Have I been to Greece,
yes or no?"

"But of course you have been to Greece! Who
would doubt it?"

"Very well! And now the red shirt: did I wear
it, yes or no?"

"But of course you did," repeated Sciarame'.

"Therefore I have been to Greece, I have
fought, I have come back. I have documents,
mind you, Sciarame', written documents to prove
all this. And now, then, according to you, what
am I?"

"Why, you are a good fellow, a nice young
man, I have already said so."

"Many thanks!" hissed La Rosa. "But that
isn't what I want to know. According to you am
I, or am I not, a Garibaldian?"

"A Garibaldian? Er . . . yes . . . why not?"
replied Sciarame', quite dazed and not knowing
where La Rosa was leading him to.

"And a veteran?" resumed the latter. "I am
also a veteran because I am not dead and have
come back. Is that right? And yet these veterans
here do not allow me to come and read the papers
of the Association because I am not a member,
isn't that so? You said it yourself. Well, I'm

going right away to find my three veteran comrades of Domokos and the four of us will, this very evening, make our formal application for membership."

"What? . . . What do you say?" replied Sciarame', opening his eyes in amazement. "You, a member here?"

"And why not?" asked Rosalino La Rosa, with a frown. "Aren't we worthy?"

"Yes, yes . . . I did not mean that. . . . Personally, I assure you, it would be an honour, a pleasure!" exclaimed Sciarame'. "But the others, you see . . . my . . . my comrades. . . ."

"I am not afraid of them, don't worry. I know that I am better entitled to be a member of this Association than someone else, do you understand, Sciarame'? And I will prove it, if they force me to do it."

Seizing him by the lapel of his coat, La Rosa gave him a good shaking; then, looking deep into his eyes, he added:

"To-night, Sciarame', do you understand?"

Stunned and shivering, Sciarame' was left standing in the centre of the room, scratching his head.

.   .   .   .

The Veterans' Association had only a little over a dozen members left, none of whom was a native of the village. Amilcare Bellone, the President, was a native of Brescia; Nardi and Navetta were from Ravenna, and in fact all of them were born in different parts of Italy, but had come to Sicily to trade in fruit or sulphur.

The Association had been formed by Bellone many years ago. At the news that Garibaldi himself was coming to Sicily to celebrate the independence of the island from foreign domination, the few Garibaldians living in the village had gathered at the café with the idea of discussing a joint trip to Palermo in order to meet—perhaps for the last time—their glorious Leader. Bellone's proposal to get together, there and then, a deputation of veterans who would—under their own flag—take part in the official procession had been greeted with genuine enthusiasm. Some of the customers at the café had brought to Bellone's notice Sciarame'—dozing as usual at one of the tables—introducing him as the old patriot of the village, a Garibaldian veteran, too. Bellone, warmed by the memory of his youthful enthusiasm and perhaps also by the wine, had gone to him, shaking him from his sleep and urging him to join the newly born Society. "Picciotto! Picciotto!"*

Enthusiasm was running high, everybody toasting and cheering. Sciarame'—amid the general shouting—had made an offer. To help the newly born Association he would allow them to instal their headquarters on the ground floor of his house, free of charge, at least temporarily, until they were able to pay their own rent. The offer had been accepted amidst general enthusiasm and from that day—forgetting that it had been merely a temporary arrangement—the veterans had stayed there for good, and paid no rent, while Sciarame', in his turn, had saved the monthly contribution of three lire paid by the others towards the cost of newspapers, magazines, light, etc. Apart from them meeting in the evenings to play cards, read the papers, talk politics or share a drink, these veterans were really giving him no trouble.

It was only now—after the President's request about Roro'—that Sciarame' had found himself between the hammer and the anvil; between an impulsive and noisy President who

*Nickname for the Sicilian volunteers, owing to their extreme youth.

would hear of no contradiction, and an obstinate girl who would listen to no reason.

"Mere children! Mere children!" shouted the President that evening, having read the application for membership from La Rosa and his friends. "Mere children, gentlemen, mere children! These brand new red shirts of recent make at three lire a yard, have only been worn once in Greece and have been brought back as clean and spotless as if they had never been used. Sit down, sit down. We shall forgo all formalities. Let the meeting decide at once; let us get rid of these children right away, with a stroke of the pen! Sit down, sit down."

But the members—all except Sciarame'—had gathered round him, asking to see the application, as though unable to believe it, and firing questions at him, especially the fat and toothless Navetta who was slightly deaf and whose wooden leg—a kind of stump round which flapped the trouser—he dragged along with almost dull, repulsive thuds.

Bellone swept them back with his arms and resumed his seat at the conference table where, ringing the bell for silence, he began to read the application aloud with endless grimaces and with comic twisting of his nose and of his lips, which sent the audience into fits of laughter.

Sciarame' alone sat quiet, his chin resting on the knob of his stick, his eyes staring at the paraffin lamp.

Having finished reading the letter, the President became solemn and dignified. Sciarame', who had stood up to speak, was quickly called to order.

"Sit down!" shouted the President.

"The lamp is smoking," retorted Sciarame', humble.

"Let it smoke! Now, gentlemen, I consider that it is idle, almost humiliating for us even to discuss such a ridiculous application" (cheers). "By a unanimous vote we shall reject—with a mere stroke of the pen—this incredible . . . this unqualifiable . . . this. . . . How shall I call it! . . ." (Bursts of applause.)

Presently Nardi asked to be allowed to speak, saying that in his opinion it was necessary and imperative to state, once and for all, that Garibaldians were only and exclusively those who had actually followed Garibaldi (Hear, hear! Hurrah! Well spoken!) Giuseppe Garibaldi, and nobody else.

"And nobody else, yes, nobody else!"

"And let us add . . ." said Navetta, suddenly springing from his seat, "let us add, gentlemen, that the . . . the, what do you call it? . . the unfortunate war between Greece and . . . and, what's the name? . . and Turkey cannot, must not be taken seriously, in view of the . . . yes, exactly, of the . . . the dreadful impression created by that nation which . . . which . . ."

"By that degenerate nation," interrupted the President, rising to his feet.

"That's the word. *Delgenerate, delgenerate*," shouted Navetta amongst the general approval.

At this moment Sciarame', who had been listening from his seat, lifted his chin from the knob of his stick and raised a hand.

"May I? . . ." he asked timidly.

Everybody turned round, frowning, while the President could not help showing his disapproval.

"You? What have *you* to say?"

Poor Sciarame' felt lost, gulped and raised his hand once more.

"You see, I should like to point out that . . . when all's said and done . . . these . . . these four young men. . . ."

"Bluffers!" snapped Bellone. "They are

bluffers and nothing else. Why, would you try to stick up for them?"

"No," Sciarame' hastened to reply. "No . . . but you see, I should like to point out, as I was saying, that . . . when all's said and done they . . . they *have* fought, these four young men: they actually *have* been in the war . . . and have shown that they were brave and fearless . . . one of them, in fact, was even wounded . . . what more do you want? That they should have all been killed? If Garibaldi, our great Leader, was not there, it was merely because he was dead, but his son was there, and it seems to me that nobody better than he had the right to wear the red shirt and to allow it to be worn by those who followed him to Greece. Therefore . . ."

To his surprise, Sciarame' had so far been allowed to speak without interruptions but now he was beginning to feel less sure of himself and less confident at the ominous silence which greeted his words. He knew quite well what it meant. He was sure that his comrades—by remaining silent—were far from approving his arguments and merely daring him to go on in order to test his stupidity or his impudence, ready to attack him at the first ill-chosen word.

He became panicky and tried to soften, little by little, the expression on his face and the tone of his voice. But soon, the words failed him as if he had said enough and the last word had been spoken in defence of those boys.

"And therefore, having regard to all this . . . I believe . . . I believe . . ."

"What do you believe?" the President interrupted at last, leaving his seat and going up to him.

"Trash! Trash!" shouted the others, also rising from their seats to hem him in, pulling him right and left and trying to convince him that he was sticking up for an unworthy cause. How could he say that those children were Garibaldians? He should be ashamed of himself—they said—for defending those four lazy rascals! Did he imagine that epics—real epics like that of Garibaldi—could have extensions and additions? Greece, he should know, had covered herself with the ridicule of the world.

They were all talking at the same time and poor Sciarame' was unable to answer them all. At random he stuck to what Nardi was saying and shouted:

"You say that the expedition was not a national

one? But, allow me, did Garibaldi, by any chance, fight exclusively for our independence? He also fought in America and even in France, always at the service of Humanity!"

"Will you be quiet, Sciarame'?" thundered Bellone at this point, with a loud bang of his fist on the conference table. "Don't make insulting comparisons! How dare you compare the Garibaldian epic with the farcical expedition to Greece? Shame! Shame! I know why you want to uphold those four buffoons, but we here to-night, you understand, with a unanimous decision will render you a service too by freeing you of a pest which threatens the honour of your family. The application of these fellows must be rejected without a single dissenting voice. Do you understand?"

"Allow me at least to stand aside . . ." begged Sciarame', joining his hands as if in prayer.

But such was their pressure and so loud were their shouts that poor Sciarame' at last agreed to cast his vote with theirs. The application was "unanimously" rejected.

.   .   .   .   .

Two days later, the following letter appeared

in the local newspaper under the signature of
Gaspari, the young fellow who had been wounded
at Domokos:

NEW AND OLD GARIBALDIANS:
Sir,
   In my own name and on behalf of my comrades
La Rosa, Betti and Marcolini, I beg to inform
you of a unanimous decision arrived at by the
Garibaldian Veterans' Association in reply to our
application for membership.

The Association has refused our application.

According to them, our red shirts are not
authentic. Just so. . . . And do you know why?
Because—as we were neither born nor even
babies when Giuseppe Garibaldi—the REAL,
the ONLY one (to use the words of the Association)—decided to fight for the freedom of the
Fatherland, we, poor fellows, could not—together
with our nurses and our mothers—follow him at
the time and we have made the mistake of following to the sacred land of the Hellenes, his son,
who (it would appear from the resolution of the
above-praised veterans) is not a Garibaldi. More-
over, we are held responsible for the sad and
humiliating end of the Greco-Turkish war, as if
we had not fought and won at Domokos, leaving
on the field the heroic Fratti and several others.

You will therefore realize, sir, how difficult
it is for us to defend our Leader, as well as the

great ideal which made us answer his call, our fallen comrades and the survivors, against the cruel offence embodied in the unqualifiable decision of these Veterans; we have no remedy because we are, unfortunately, faced by old men obviously in their dotage. These words may seem hard, Sir, but are justified by the fact that these men have rejected our application while harbouring amongst their members, *a man who has not only never been a Garibaldian and has never taken part in any actual fighting, but actually wears a red shirt and pins to his breast no less than seven medals which do not belong to him but to his brother, heroically killed at Dijon.*

Having said this much, I deem it superfluous to make any further comment on the Association's decision. I am ready to prove, with the support of undeniable evidence, all I have written above. If necessary, I shall also give the name of this false Garibaldian who even had the audacity of voting with the others against our admission.

In the meantime, I beg to remain, Sir,

Yours, etc.

ALESSANDRO GASPARI.

The letter was followed by a short note by the Editor.

"We have been aware for some considerable time that one of the members of the Association

214

of Garibaldian Veterans had never fought with Garibaldi or even seen him. We have always refrained from revealing this fact out of pity for an old man, but owing to the incredible step taken by the above-mentioned Association in refusing the application of Signor Gaspari and his brave companions who fought in Greece, we consider that the Association should at least give some satisfaction to these young men and safe-guard its own reputation by urging the resignation of a member who appears to be totally unworthy of belonging to it."

The entire village was puzzled, everyone commenting on Gaspari's unexpected protest. Sciarame' was about to leave his home for the piazza, when Bellone—a copy of the paper in his hand—rushed to him, pushing him into a chair and holding the paper under his nose.

"Have you read it?" he asked. "Read this!"

"No . . . what . . . what has happened?" muttered Sciarame', unable to understand the outburst.

"Read! Read!" yelled Bellone, clenching his fists to control himself, and pacing the room like a lion.

Sciarame' fumbled for his glasses, placing them on the tip of his nose and wondering what

he was supposed to read in that paper. Bellone
came up to him, tearing it from his hands and
pointing to the letter which appeared on the
second page.

"Here! here! Read here!"

"Ah!" said the other sadly, after a quick glance
at the headline and the signature. "Didn't I
tell you?"

"Go on! go on! Read!" again yelled Bellone,
more furious than ever.

Sciarame' began to read, at times knitting his
brows, at times smoothing them out again, then
staring with his mouth wide open as if staggered.
The paper nearly fell from his hands. He grasped
it more firmly bringing it closer to his eyes as
though his sight had suddenly failed him. The
President was now watching him, his eyes
flaming, his arms folded, waiting for a protest, a
denial or an explanation.

"What have you to say about it? Lift up your
head! Look at me!"

Sciarame', his face deadly pale and his eyelids
hanging heavily over his weary eyes, shook his
head slowly, unable to speak: he placed the
paper on the table and brought a hand to his
heart.

"Wait . . ." he finally said, more with his gesture than with his voice.

He tried hard to swallow, but his tongue was dry and swollen. His breathing had become heavy.

"I . . ." he feebly murmured, "I . . . I *was* there . . . at . . . at Calatafimi . . . and at . . . at . . . Palermo . . . at Milazzo . . . and in Calabria at . . . at Melito . . . then right up to . . . to Naples . . . and the Volturno. . . ."

"But how were you there? What proofs can you give?"

"Wait . . . I . . . together with my brother . . . I followed him with the donkey. . . ."

"What are you raving about? The medals, I want to know, whose are they? Yours or your brother's? Speak up!"

"I was . . . let me explain. . . . At Marsala . . . we were there together, my little brother Stefanuccio and I . . . I had been acting as a father to him. . . . He was barely fifteen, you see? He ran way from me when . . . when the glorious 'Thousand' landed there . . . to follow him, Garibaldi, along with the other volunteers. . . . I came home; I found my brother had gone. . . . So I hired a donkey . . . I made up my mind to bring Stefanuccio back. . . . I caught him up before he had reached Calatafimi. . . . At fifteen years of age of what good could he have been to the Leader, I ask you? . . . But he threatened to . . . to blow his own head off with an old rifle—twice his size—which they had given him, if I forced him to return. . . . Yes, his own head. . . . Then, listening to the advice of the other volunteers, I let the donkey free . . . for which I had to pay later on . . . and . . . and I decided to join them too."

"As a volunteer also? And did you fight?"

"I . . . I hadn't a rifle."

"And in fact you hadn't the courage?"

"No . . . no . . . I would have rather died than leave my brother."

"So you followed him."

"Yes, everywhere."

And Sciarame', feeling a shiver down his back, pressed his hand a little firmer against his heart.

"But the medals? The red shirt?" resumed Bellone, trembling with rage. "Whose are they? Yours or your brother's? Answer me!"

Sciarame' extended his arms without daring to lift his head; then he said:

"My brother was dead . . . and could not enjoy them any more . . . so I thought. . . ."

"You decided to show them off, instead!" The President finished the sentence for him. "Oh, you wretched impostor! Cheat! I could spit at your face! You deserve to be. . . . But I will have pity on you. Out you go from the Association; out you go, at once!"

"What? You want to turn me out of my own house?"

"No, we shall go away ourselves, right now! Have the plate removed! How blind I was not to see that a fool like you could never have seen Garibaldi—even at a distance!"

"Never seen him, you say?" shouted Sciarame' with a jerk. "Never seen him? I'll tell you whether I saw him or not! I even kissed his hands! I kissed them on the piazza Pretorio at Palermo, where he had set his camp."

"Shut up, scoundrel. I don't want to listen to you any longer. I don't want to see you any more! Remove the plate and heaven help you if I ever see you wearing the red shirt again."

He made for the door, but once more turned round to yell:

"Cheat! Cheat!"

Left alone, Sciarame' tried to rise to his feet, but his legs were unsteady and trembling. Clinging first to the table, then to the chair and to the railing, he carried himself heavily upstairs.

Roro', seeing him in such a state, gave a cry: but he motioned to her to be quiet: then, pointing to the chest-of-drawers in the room, he begged her in a half-choked voice:

"The papers?" "What papers?" implored Roro', trying to help him.

"My papers . . . my brother's . . ." muttered Sciarame', dragging himself to the chest-of-drawers. "Open it. . . . Let me look. . . ."

Roro' opened the drawer. Sciarame' laid a trembling hand on a bundle of soiled, faded documents tied together with a string, and then turned to his step-daughter with lifeless eyes:

"Did you . . . did you show them to . . . to La Rosa?" he asked. At first Roro' could make no reply: then, anxious and scared, she said:

"He asked me to see them. . . . What harm have I done?"

Breaking into wild sobs, Sciarame' collapsed in her arms. With difficulty Roro' dragged him to the chair at the foot of the bed and made him sit down.

"Daddy! Daddy!" she implored. "What is it? What have I done? Why are you crying? What has happened?"

"Go . . . go away . . . leave me alone!" gasped Sciarame', choking. "And to think that I stood up for them . . . I alone . . . and this is their gratitude! I *was* there . . . with him. . . . He was only fifteen. . . . There was the donkey, too . . . then at the first shots . . . my legs . . . my legs. . . . No, I was not afraid. . . . And later at Milazzo . . . concealed amongst the vineyards. . . ."

Roro' was watching him, unable to understand.

"Daddy . . . Daddy . . . what are you saying?"

But Sciarame', his eyes wide and lifeless, his face contorted, a hand pressed on his heart, no longer heard her words.

He was looking back, far back, into the past.

He really *had* followed him, that little brother of his to whom he had been a second father; he really *had* caught him up, on his donkey, before they had reached Calatafimi, imploring him with joined hands to come back home, and not to make him die of sorrow at the thought of leaving him alone in such grave danger. It had all been in vain, so that he had had to give way and little by little, fired by the general enthusiasm—he had

221

himself followed the others. Then, when the first shots had been fired. . . . No, no, even then he was never really sorry to have let the donkey go. Would he have ever gone back knowing that his young brother was in the thick of a battle and perhaps on the verge of being mercilessly killed? On the contrary, he had felt like rushing to his help and throwing himself into the battle too, but his legs, his legs had failed him. What can a poor man do when he is no longer master of his legs? Nothing but wait and suffer. God alone knew how much he had suffered. He had suffered for two: for himself and for his brother. . . . Then, when the battle was over, he had searched the field trying to find his little Stefanuccio amongst the dead and the wounded. . . . But no. . . . Stefanuccio was alive and well! From that day, he had followed him everywhere, first to Palermo, as far as Gibilrossa, where he had waited for him, more dead than alive, for endless days: an eternity! At Palermo, Stefanuccio —as a reward for his bravery—had been allowed to join the Carabineers, a famous regiment which was later almost annihilated in the battle of Milazzo. It was really a miracle that he too— Sciarame'—had not been killed on that day.

Squatting in a vineyard he could occasionally hear—on all sides—strange thuds among the foliage; but never once had it dawned on him that they might be bullets, when suddenly, amongst the branches of the vines he was crouching against. . . . Ah! that dreadful hiss before the thud! Flattened on the ground, shivering with fear, he had tried to move away, but in vain; and he had stopped there, in agony, amid the deluge of bullets, facing death at every thud.

Who could dare to say that he had not known all the horrors of war? Who could dare to say that the stories he was so fond to relate had not been seen and lived by him? Yes, he *had* been in the war even if he had not actually fought in it. Back in his village, after Garibaldi's gift of the Two Sicilies to King Victor-Emmanuel, he had been hailed as a hero along with his brother Stefanuccio. As to the medals, however, his brother alone had received them, but in a way didn't they belong to them both? . . . Besides, he had never boasted about them: when he had been asked to speak, he had always talked on something he had actually seen, nothing else. Never—never indeed—would he have dreamt of joining the Association had he not been almost forced to do so on that eventful night at the café, when he had found himself a member almost against his will. He had reciprocated the honour bestowed upon him (an honour of which he was really not altogether unworthy) by giving them shelter, rent free, during all those years. Yes, perhaps it was wrong to wear his brother's shirt and to decorate his breast with medals which—strictly speaking—were not his own; but, having once made the first step, how could he possibly withdraw? He simply had to keep on, being satisfied at the thought that—at all events—he was representing his poor little brother, now dead, killed in battle at Dijon, his poor little Stefanuccio who so well deserved those medals and yet had never been able to wear them at a single ceremony.

This—if a sin it was—had been his only one. Those new Garibaldians had been the cause of all the trouble; they had quarrelled with the old ones; and *he* had been their victim, he who had stood up for them, one against them all. Ah, the ungrateful creatures! They had killed him!

Roro', frightened at the ghastly, lifeless expression of his face, rushed to the window shouting for help.

A few of the neighbours hurried to her assistance.

"What is it? What is it?"

At the sight of Sciarame', sunk in his chair, they stood still.

Two of them, bolder than the others, took him by his shoulders and feet, trying to lift him on his bed. They had only just laid him down when. . . .

"God! . . ." said one.

"Look! . . ." said the other.

"Dead? . . ." asked someone from behind.

For a second Roro' was stunned, her wide eyes staring at him, helplessly. Then, turning to the neighbours who had answered her call, she muttered:

"God! . . . Dead? . . . Really *dead*?"

And, throwing herself over her step-father's body, her head bent low and her arms stretched out over the corpse, she knelt by the bed.

"Forgive me, Daddy! Forgive me! . . ."

The neighbours were puzzled. Forgive her? Why? What had she done? Why—in her sobs —was she speaking of papers and documents? What documents? They tore her away from the bed and dragged her into her own room. While some of them went to fetch the President others remained to watch beside the bed.

When the President arrived—dark and concerned—with Navetta, Nardi and the other members, old Sciarame' was lying on his little bed, wearing his red shirt, with the seven medals pinned to his breast.

The neighbours had thought it right to bury the old man in the red shirt of which he was so proud. It didn't belong to him? What then? Worse lies than this have been written on many graves. On with the medals! Let all seven of them be pinned to his breast!

Thud, thud, thud. Navetta—the man with the wooden leg—came near the corpse. For a while he stood by in silence, then turning to his comrades and in a hollow voice:

"Shall we take them off?" he said.

The President—who had retired to confabulate with the others in a corner of the room—called him with a sign of his hand. Then, shrugging his shoulders as if to show that he was merely expressing the opinion of his members, he ordered:

"Leave them on. . . . He is dead. . . ."

They gave him a magnificent funeral.

BITTER WATERS

Not many people that morning in the Pump Room grounds, the season coming near its end. Under the chestnut-trees two men were sitting on two separate benches, each holding in his hand a glass filled with the tepid and bitter water from the spring. One of them, young and pale-looking—(his face was almost yellow)—was so thin that from his bones the immaculate grey suit hung like a concertina, while the other—a stout fellow in his 'fifties—with a shapeless panama on his bald head—seemed at pains to prevent his colossal fatness from bursting through his tight-fitting and badly wrinkled linen suit.

Every now and then the fat man (his round and happy-looking face recalled the image of a Father Abbot) would droop his heavy eyelids as if still not fully awake, while the young man, obviously feeling the sting of the autumn air, looked cold and shivery.

Neither of them seemed willing to take the first

sip, each one waiting for the other's lead. At last, after a first taste, they looked at each other with the same expression of disgust:

"Nasty stuff!" said the fat man, leaning towards the other. "Hepatic colic, too, I suppose? But, excuse my asking, you are a bachelor, aren't you?"

"Yes. But why?" retorted the young man with a grin intended as a smile.

"Because . . . because if you are not married these waters will do you a lot of good."

"And what about you, are you married?" enquired the young man in his turn, turning sharply to his neighbour.

"Married? No, thank God. I no longer have a wife or a liver disease. I got rid of both of them thirteen years ago. It is merely out of gratitude that I come back here, once a year. But when did you arrive?"

"Last night, at dinner-time."

"Now I understand," said the fat fellow, slowly shaking his head. "Had you arrived during the day you would already know who I am."

"Why? Are you so popular, then?"

"I should think so. I am a famous person here.

BITTER WATERS

For the last thirteen years everyone has been talking of me on the Piazza, in the cafés, in the hotels, at the club and even at the chemist's shop. I enjoy it and that's why I keep on coming. Where are you staying? At the Grand? Well, you can be sure that everyone will want to tell you my story, so perhaps I had better give it to you myself before you get a wrong version of it. . . . May I?"

He lifted himself laboriously from his bench and sank heavily on the other bench, next to the young man.

.   .   .   .   .

"First of all, although everyone here called me 'Carlotta's husband' my real name is Cambie', Bernard Cambie', or 'Fat Bernard' because I am fat.

"Have a sip. I'll have one too."

They both sipped, their faces contracting to the usual grin which soon changed into a smile.

"You are very young," continued the fat man, "and very liverish: therefore I hope that the story I am going to tell you will help towards your recovery more than this bitter water which, although very nasty, doesn't do much good, believe me. We drink it because we believe in it, as we believe many lies which are served to us as the truth. . . . If these waters were really so good . . . but no, you are here for the cure; I must not destroy your faith in them.

"Coming back to my story," he continued. "I must tell you that when I was young the mere word 'marriage' used to make me sick. . . . Yes, sir, real sickness . . . turning my stomach upside down. Seeing a honeymoon couple or hearing that a friend was going to get married, was enough for me: I simply couldn't help it. Small events are often the cause of important effects. A tiny spot of the sun may set alive a dead volcano: the illness of a king may stir up a war. In the same way marriage was upsetting me. I was living in Naples with my family when the plague broke out, the terrible plague of which you have no doubt heard, although you are very young. My father—with his usual luck—had just been given a post in town and the whole family had settled down there, myself included. To tell the truth, I was not staying with them, but was living on my own in a small flat near theirs. There was a girl too, you understand—Carlotta.

"She was the daughter of a usurer, an unfrocked priest into the bargain, and had run away from home to escape from a quarrelsome mother and a rascally brother. Not a bad girl—I thought at the time—but of course I was seeing her through a lover's eyes, as I found out afterwards.

"Now tell me, sir, do you believe in religion? Half and half, I suppose, like myself. My mother, on the contrary, who was soaked in religion, could find no peace at the idea that I was living with a woman who was not my wife and when the plague broke out, feeling certain that we would all die (especially those who were living in sin) demanded that I should at once marry this girl.

"Believe me, I would have never agreed to it had the girl not fallen suddenly ill and had I not promised my brother to rescue Carlotta's soul before it was too late. I hastily summoned a priest and married her. But what happened? Was it a miracle? She was near death but she recovered. My mother who, out of charity, had witnessed the ceremony, nursed her for days and nights like her own child, even insisting on taking her home where she was convalescent, against my own will.

"It was a great mistake, sir, the greatest of all mistakes. But let's have another sip."

"Fortunately Carlotta's family—father, mother and brother—all died during the epidemic. Fortunately and unfortunately, because the few thousand lire which Carlotta inherited from her father's noble profession made a complete and disastrous change in her. In less than a few weeks she had not only become my wife but also a wife with money, which was far worse.

"Now, listen. Perhaps you may think I am a little bit of a phil . . . of a philosopher and you may find it funny, but let me explain to you. Do you think there are only two genders, masculine and feminine? If so you are wrong! A wife is a gender of its own and so is a husband, with the difference that the woman always gains by marriage. She pushes through and succeeds in absorbing such a large portion of the masculine gender that she always scores while the husband suffers and loses pretty heavily.

"Were I to write a grammar I would insist on ruling 'wife' as masculine and 'husband' as feminine.

"You laugh? In the wife's eyes, dear sir, the husband is no longer a man, so much so that she does not even try to be attractive to him. 'Why should I?' she seems to say. 'You know me well enough.' Yet if the husband is silly enough to pass a remark when he sees her in bed with her hair in curlers and her face smeared with grease she is quite sure to protest: 'Fool, don't you see I am doing it for you?'

" 'For me?'

" 'Of course for you, so that you may be proud of going out with a beautiful wife. Would you like to hear people pity you when we go out together: 'Poor man, fancy choosing such an awful-looking woman for his wife'?

"And the husband who—believe me—is no longer a man, takes it in without an answer while he ought to make a stand and yell at her: 'Other people pity me? But don't you see that I should pity myself for seeing you near me in such a state? You want me to stand all this so that people in the street may find you beautiful? So that they may envy me? Why don't you speak the truth and say that you do all this not because of me but because of yourself, because you want people to look at you and admire you? Why this false charity because I was silly enough to marry you?'

"Of course, the discussion could be carried on still further as the wife might go as far as to ask her husband's advice on whether a certain hat or a dress suits her.

" 'It all depends,' might say the husband, 'according to taste. Whom do you want to please? Nobody in particular? In which case, my dear, you might just as well try to please me and start by changing the way you dress your hair.'

"Don't laugh, my dear sir, and just think what the wife would do. She would look at her husband with pitiful eyes shrugging her shoulders:

" 'To please you? But what concern of yours is it, whichever way I dress my hair?'

"And she would be right. After all, it's purely a matter of instinct and women—by instinct—must make themselves attractive to others: they must be admired, they must cause other people to desire them: they are not happy otherwise, believe me.

"Now—you understand—no husband can, after a certain time, feel towards his wife in the same way as she would like him to feel for ever, with the result that to her he is no longer the Man, while to him she is no longer the Woman.

"What is the outcome of all this? The outcome is that while the man—who is a philosopher by nature—puts up with it, the woman gets resentful and finds the husband dull and unbearable.

"In other words, the woman may do what she likes, but the husband, no.

"Besides, whatever the man did would be wrong because, for the mere fact of his being her husband—he would be unable to surround her with that particular atmosphere of admiration which she needs. Admiration! Where does the admiration come in when the husband sees his wife running about the house with curlers in her hair, wearing slippers or perhaps even down for stomach- or tooth-ache? Only strangers, men who don't know her, may provide this atmosphere of admiration and fall prey to her attractions. This —in the case of a virtuous wife—is enough; in the case of a different woman...but I had better not speak of them. What is certain is that while we, men, keep on saying that woman is above all understanding we are utterly wrong. Woman is not different from man; the only difference being that she dare neither show it nor acknowledge it for fear of social prejudice and also because she knows that men do not like her to say so. This is the whole enigma. Whoever—

like myself—has come across a wife who is not afraid of letting her tongue loose knows it well, believe me. Now let's have another sip. . . . It's good for the liver."

.   .   .   .   .

"To come back to my story, I must say that Carlotta wasn't like that at first. She changed after her marriage, when she felt that, having become my wife, I was beginning to see in her not merely a pleasure but also a duty. Having married her I was bound to respect her and it was this respect which annoyed her most. To see me change from a lover to an ideal husband upset her to the point that our married life soon began to be hell. She, always sulky, touchy, restless. I, always patient and submissive partly from fright and partly because I soon realized the terrible mistake I had made and the heavy consequences I would have to face from this marriage. I was following her round like a puppy, trying to understand what she really wanted. But can you guess what it was she wanted? She wanted to have been born a man and she was angry with me because she had been born a woman.

"One day I asked her:

" 'But what would you have been, had you been born a man?'

" 'A crook,' she fired back, staring at me with defiant eyes.

" 'Fine!'

" 'And I would never have married, believe me!'

" 'Thanks, dear!'

" 'No, never, I am quite sure.'

" 'But why?'

"My wife's eyes became even more fiery: 'Because I would not have liked to make a prisoner of an unfortunate woman.'

" 'A prisoner?' I said. 'A prisoner? Do you feel like a prisoner here then?'

" 'I *feel*? I *am*. What have I always been if not a prisoner; since I was born, since I met you? When have I ever been free?'

" 'You mean free to lead your own life.'

" 'Yes, of course, as free as you have been to meet other women when they took your fancy.'

"This proves, sir, as I was telling you before, that there is no difference between Man and Woman and that a woman's feelings are exactly the same as those of a man.

"But let's have another sip."

·   ·   ·   ·   ·

"It was only natural that after a year of married life I should develop a liver.

"For six consecutive years I tried all possible cures, but instead of recovering I was getting worse and worse.

"At last I came here, where the remedy was found. I came with my wife, staying at the Grand; the same place where you are. I sent for a doctor to examine me and prescribe the treatment. He turned out to be a tall, dark, handsome-looking young man, with a peculiar military appearance. I learnt later that he had been a doctor in the army, and after an affair with a young girl whom his father had compelled him to marry, had had to resign from the army and had started to practise here. Some eight months later both wife and child had died and although more than three years had passed he was still mourning them, wearing nothing but black, like a proud and beautiful crow.

"The fact that his army career had been ruined for sake of love, and that his sacrifice had been so badly rewarded by fate, had made him immensely popular. Women, above all, seemed to be eager to console him, but he treated them with contempt.

"This was the fellow who came to see me, tapping me all over, telling me more or less what other doctors had told me before and prescribing me the treatment: three half glasses of the water for the first few days and then three full glasses daily. A bath and a shower an alternate days. He was almost leaving the room when he pretended to notice my wife.

" 'Your wife, too?' he said, looking at her coldly.

" 'No, not me,' she replied, with a drawn face.

" 'All the same,' he insisted, 'allow me.'

"He came up to her, gently raising her chin with the left hand and slightly lifting an eyelid with a finger of the other hand.

" 'Slight anæmia,' he said.

"My wife looked at me, pale and haggard, as if the abrupt diagnosis had really made her anæmic; then, with a slight shrug of her shoulders she tried to smile at the doctor:

" 'Yet I feel perfectly well,' she said.

"The doctor made a ceremonious bow.

" 'So much the better,' he answered, leaving the room.

.   .   .   .   .

"Whether it was the waters or the shower or the bath or perhaps—as I believe—the invigorating air of the Tuscan hills, the fact remained that I felt better almost at once, so well, indeed, that I decided to stop here one or two months and rented a small house close to the hotel, a house with a fine balcony overlooking the magnificent valley with its two lakes.

"Then—perhaps you have already guessed it —it was my wife's turn to fall ill. She didn't call it anæmia, as the doctor had done, but a tired feeling of her heart and a sense of oppression on her chest which prevented her from breathing freely.

"Trying to look as concerned as possible I asked her:

" 'Shall I ask the doctor to examine you?'

"Of course, she refused furiously—as I had foreseen—but from day to day she grew worse until one day—seeing that I was taking no notice of her—she agreed that a doctor's visit was necessary, but not that doctor, oh! no, she would rather have his old colleague, the asthmatic and almost blind Dr. Berri, already half retired and now almost completely ready for his final retirement to the other world.

" 'Nonsense,' I said, 'Who calls Dr. Berri any more? Besides, it would be an insult to our own doctor who has always shown himself so obliging with us.'

"It was true, I forgot to tell you that since our arrival the young doctor would come and greet us every morning at the Pump Room, congratulating me on my improvement, walking up and down the park with us and always behaving with great respect towards my wife, although talking so little to her, at first, that, though she kept silent, I knew she was bursting with rage.

"Then, after a week, my wife had begun to argue with him on the eternal question of Man and Woman, on Man who wants all his freedom and Woman who is the eternal victim, on the injustice of the social world, etc., the usual stories which—for seven years—had formed the daily arguments of our married life.

"Although I had heard quite enough of them, I must confess that I was really amused to hear the young doctor answer her arguments with almost my own words, seasoned with all the salt and pepper of his scientific knowledge. When addressing me she had covered me with insults but now—hearing the same things from the doctor—she had to keep up appearances and be content with coating each word with the bile of which she was so full.

"I was hoping, therefore, that her heart disease would improve, but nothing of the kind. On the contrary she grew worse and worse, a clear sign— don't you agree?—that she wanted to try new arguments to win over her man. And just imagine the comic role a husband has to play at times. I knew perfectly well that what my wife really wanted was to be visited by that young doctor and that her pretended dislike for him and her own disease were nothing but comedy, yet I had to play my part to the end and spend hours convincing her to do the very thing she wanted to do.

"Don't laugh, sir, and listen. When my wife stretched herself on the bed and the doctor looked into her eyes while bending over her to test her heart, I saw her almost swooning, almost collapsing. I knew her so well . . . I could not be mistaken.

"So far nothing wrong. Merely a medical examination of a perfectly honest wife with the husband looking on. But then—I ask—what made that man come and sing, under my very nose, something which I already knew quite well, something I had always seen with my own eyes and almost touched with my own hand?

"Come, come, let's forget. Another sip, sir, shall we?"

.　　　.　　　.　　　.　　　.

"One night, I was leaning over the balcony admiring the wide valley below me, beautifully bathed in moonlight.

"My wife was already in bed.

"Because I am so fat people think I cannot be affected by nature's beauty, yet, believe me, sir, my soul is so sensitive, so soft and tender that— when it peeps at the world through these great bullock's eyes—it cannot help being moved at the sight of the moon or even at the ringing of the bells in the fields.

"Men by day in the cities and grasshoppers by night in the fields never seem to rest. Fine profession, a grasshopper's.

"What's your job?"

"Singing."

"Why singing? He doesn't know. He sings, that's all. And why do the stars flicker in the sky? What are they doing up there? Nothing.

Just looking down through space in an endless
shiver. And what about the owl, surrounded by
all this enchantment, suddenly bursting in sobs,
from afar, as if in anguish. Why does he cry?
Because he is moved too. . . .

"But let's go back to that night. It was past
eleven, the air was getting chilly and I was
beginning to retire to my bedroom when suddenly I heard a prolonged and loud knocking at
the street door. Who could be knocking at that
hour?

"It was the doctor, in such a state, my dear sir,
as to make you feel sorry for him: drunk as a lord.
Five or six of his colleagues had arrived from the
neighbouring towns and he—together with the
chemist—had got up a dinner in their honour
which had sent them home drunk.

"But what made him come to my house, instead
of going home too, and upset my dreams of that
wonderful night?

"I got out of the house trying to hold him up
and prevent him falling in the street. He threw
both arms round my neck, assuring me that he
loved me, loved me like a brother and had been
speaking all night about me and my illness with
his colleagues; in fact, he had come round to see

me, for to-morrow he might not be at the Pump
Room. He had been drinking a little too much
that night, he was sure.

"I pretended to be grateful for his visit and
begged him to go home, before it got too late.
Nothing doing: he asked for a chair and went on
talking about my wife, the dear little Carlotta,
whom he liked so much too. Would I go and
wake her up? She would be only too pleased to
come down and see him. Hadn't she fallen in
love with him? Of course she had! . . . And
how well she pretended to be ill so as to get him
near her. . . . And so on and so on, laughing
and cunningly winking his eyes.

"Now, sir, I ask you, what could I do to a
man in that condition? Could I thrash somebody
who could hardly stand on his feet? That's what
my wife (who had awakened in the meantime)
was yelling me to do from her bedroom. But how
could I? What else could I do to that idiot who
—through the blessed unconsciousness of wine
—had lost all sense of social conventions and was
merrily spitting the truth in my face?

"I begged him to go and at last—getting hold
of him as best I could—I lifted him from his
chair and took him to the edge of the road: there,

I admit, but only there I gave him a slight push which sent him rolling to the ground.

"When I went back, my wife was in a real fury, almost in hysterics. She had got up from bed and started covering me with the most violent insults. Had I been another man, she said, I would have trampled on that brute and thrown him from the window: I was a puppet, a man without any feeling, any pride, unable to defend a wife's honour, quite capable of throwing her into the arms of. . . .

"I didn't let her finish. I raised a hand, threatening to thrash her as I would have thrashed the man, had he not been drunk. I begged her to stop. But did she stop? On the contrary. She went on and on. Her fury changed into scoffing. Of course I was trying to bully a woman instead of thrashing a man who had insulted me on my very doorstep. Why hadn't I told her he was there? Why hadn't I led him politely to her room?

" 'You must challenge him to a duel,' she yelled at last, mad with rage, 'you must challenge him, or God help you!'

"When a woman behaves like this every man has the right to revolt. So did I. I got into bed swearing that I would not challenge anyone, if only so as not to give her that satisfaction.

"But all that night I could not sleep, thinking over and over again what had happened. I knew nothing—and I still don't know anthing—about the Code of Honour; whether the insult of a man under the influence of drink, a man who does not know what he is saying, can be sufficient cause for a duel. I decided therefore that on the following morning I would consult an ex-army officer whom I had met at the Pump Room, but when the morning came and I was making ready to leave my house, this very man, accompanied by a friend, called on me. They had been sent by the doctor to challenge me to a duel for the way I had dealt with him on the previous night, causing a wound on his nose.

" 'But he was drunk,' I yelled at the two gentlemen.

" 'All the worse for me,' they said. I should have been all the more careful. Now you see the comedy of it all? I was forced to a duel for having gently pushed that man on the road while my wife had nearly killed me because I had not trampled on him and thrown him out of the window!

"To cut it short I accepted the challenge, but my wife laughed at the news with contempt. She immediately began to pack her trunk, even without waiting for the result of the duel, although she knew that the conditions were extremely grave.

"As I have to fight, let it be a real fight, I thought. He had the right to choose the weapon; he chose pistols. Very well, then; it will be at fifteen paces, no more, I claimed on my turn. And being certain of my death I wrote a letter that now makes me laugh whenever I read it again. It's incredible the nonsense a man can write on the eve of his death. . . .

"I had never handled firearms before and I swear that—when my turn came—I shut my eyes when pulling the trigger. The duel was fought in a quiet corner of the great wood. The first two shots went wide . . . the third . . . no, the third too went wide: it was at the fourth, yes, at the fourth shot (he was a hard-headed fellow that doctor) that the bullet took its own aim and went right to his forehead, luckily missing the bone and scraping along the top.

"Everybody thought he was dead: we all rushed to him, but one of my seconds urged me to jump into a carriage and run away as fast as I could.

"I followed his advice and escaped.

"It was only on the following day that I got news of the man and that I also learnt something which filled me with joy and regret, joy for myself and regret for my opponent, who really deserved better luck after that bullet in the head. Do you know what the doctor—who had been brought to the Green Cross Hospital—saw when he opened his eyes after his long spell of unconsciousness? He saw—sitting at his bedside—my wife, who had rushed to nurse him.

"Poor man . . . of his wound he was cured in less than a fortnight; of my wife, my dear sir, he has never been cured.

"Shall we now go for another glass?"

A CAT, A FINCH AND THE STARS

A STONE. And yet another stone. We pass by and we see them together. But what does this stone know of the other which lies next to it? Or what do the flowing waters know of the river-bed? We see the river and its bed: we hear the waters flow and we almost imagine that, in their swift course, they are sharing their secrets with the river-bed.

Ah, what a night of stars on the roofs of this little village lost in the mountains. Gazing at the sky from the roofs one could swear that the stars, to-night, have eyes for nothing else but these roofs, so brightly do they shine upon them.

Yet what interest do the stars take in the earth?

And those mountains? Can they ignore too that they belong to the little village buried among them for almost a thousand years? Everyone knows their names, Mount Corno, Mount Moro; yet they alone seem to ignore their very existence. And what of this old house, standing at the crossroads? Does it ignore, too, why it was built at that very place?

If you believe it is so, you may as well believe that on that night the stars had only eyes for the roofs of the little village lost among the mountains.

Once, in that little village, lived an old couple who had a finch. Never had it entered their heads that the little bird—gazing at them, at his cage, or at the old-fashioned house—could see all this through different eyes than their own. In fact they were quite sure that the little bird was quite able to choose between grandfather's or grandmother's shoulder upon which to perch when flying down from his cage and also that he knew quite well that their attentions for him were out of love for their little niece, now dead, who had nursed him and trained him so cleverly.

Only at night would the little beggar return to his cage, hung between the curtains by the window. In the day-time he would prefer to fly about the room, returning to his cage only to peck at his millet or to sip a few drops of water. In a way the cage was his palace while the room was his vast empire. Often he would perch on the lampshade of the dining-room or even on the back of grandfather's arm-chair pouring forth his

merry song and even . . . well, you know what
birds are. . . .

"Dirty boy," Grandma would scold when she
saw him misbehave. And she would hurry along
with a rag always kept handy for emergencies,
unable to forget that—until a year ago—it was
Maria, her little niece, who would hurry with the
same rag when the little bird misbehaved. Poor
little Maria, poor little darling . . . so young, so
good, so friendly with her little finch. . . .

"Do you remember. . . ?"

Did he remember. . . . Why, he could still see
her running about the house, just a tiny mite,
no taller than that. . . . And the old man would
slowly shake his head.

They had been left alone, those two, alone
with the little orphan who had slowly grown under
their care and who was to have been the joy of
their old age. But instead, at fifteen. . . . Her
memory alone had survived, kept alive by that
little finch with its trills and its wings. Neither
Grandfather nor Grandmother had paid any
attention to the little animal at first, so deeply
were they buried in their tragic grief, but one day
the finch had flown from its little cage, to perch on
grandfather's shoulder—still shaken with sobs—

and turning its little head this way and that, had stretched its neck to peck at an ear, quite gently, as if anxious to explain that . . . yes, that it was a living part of her and still needed the same love, the same care, which they had shown her.

Ah, how the old man's clumsy hand had trembled when he had caught the little finch and shown it to his old woman, still unable to restrain his sobs. How they both covered that tiny head with their kisses. But freedom was what the little bird was asking for, struggling with its feet and its head, returning nippings for kisses.

Grandmother was certain—oh yes, quite certain—that the little finch's song was meant for his dead young mistress and that his flights round the room were merely secret messages to her, messages which no word could have more clearly expressed, messages repeated three or four consecutive times as if the bird were expecting an answer and were getting impatient at receiving none.

But why, wondered grandfather, who never doubted that the little bird was aware of the girl's death? Why? Why should he sing and fly about? Whom was he calling and whom did he expect to answer his messages?

A CAT, A FINCH AND THE STARS

Well, good gracious, it was only a finch, after all. One moment he would call her and the next he would mourn her. For instance, as he sat nestled up inside his cage, his tiny head sunk into his shoulders, his beak in the air, his eyes half closed, could one possibly doubt that he was thinking of his young mistress? Now and again he would heave a sigh, short and weary; wasn't that a proof that he was mourning her, feeling sad at having been left alone? How painful those sighs were.

The old man could not say that his wife was wrong. In fact he was so sure of it that he would get up and stand on his chair to get nearer the cage and whisper a few words of comfort to the little bird in its misery. Then, almost unconsciously, he would open the door of the cage which had been shut, letting the little bird fly again into the room.

"Here he runs again, the little beggar," he would say, turning round to follow it in its flight.

But grandmother would not agree. Why had he upset the little animal again? Why couldn't he leave it alone in its grief? Couldn't he hear how the little one was complaining?

"Complaining? He is singing."

"No, complaining, I tell you. He is just telling you how nasty you are not to leave him alone."

And she would run after the little creature, trying to soothe him, but did the finch want to be soothed? He was springing right and left, restless and angry. Quite right too: could he be anything but angry, feeling that they had treated him without consideration?

"He is right, perfectly right," the old man would say. "He feels that nobody takes any interest in him."

Poor old man! Didn't he know only too well what it meant to be treated without consideration? Wasn't he grieved to see neighbours treating him and his wife without consideration, laughing at them for keeping their windows latched day and night out of devotion to a little bird? Wasn't he grieved to see them scoffing at him because he would hardly go out and would prefer to stay at home with his old woman and the finch, often crying like a child? Yes, they were most inconsiderate and cruel, but—beware—even at his age he was not going to allow anyone to make fun of him or of his finch, and if anyone dared. . . .

And boiling with rage he would get up from

his chair, the finch on his shoulder, staring with angry eyes at the houses opposite.

Houses, roofs, windows, balconies, flowers, chimneys, tiles and gutters: this is what grand-father could see. He knew every house, almost every brick, every neighbour. But was it the same for the finch perched on his shoulder or for the beautiful cat—the snow-white persian—squatting on one of the windows across the road, his eyes shut, basking in the sun?

Windows? Tiles? Roofs? His house? Other people's houses? What did it matter to the cat whether this was his house or somebody else's? To him weren't all houses alike, merely places where he could go and steal or sleep or pretend to be asleep? . . .

Did those two old fools across the road really believe that even if they kept the front door and the windows locked day and night a cat would not find his way in, once he had made up his mind to eat the finch?

And wasn't it too much for that old man to pretend that the cat should know that the little finch was the whole world for him and his wife? How was the cat to know that grandfather had called on its mistress and threatened to shoot it if he had caught it again spying at the little bird through the pane of the window with the obvious intent of a good meal?

Well, it so happened that one day the cat ate the finch, yes, that very finch which to him was no more than an ordinary bird. Nobody ever knew how he managed to get inside the house. Grandmother—it was almost dusk—heard a tiny squeak, a whining, far away, from the dining-room. Nothing more. Grandfather rushed to the place and half-saw a white object hurrying through the room towards the kitchen door and leaving behind a few light feathers—those of the breast—still floating in the air. What a cry! It seemed as if grandfather had suddenly gone insane and nothing—not even grandmother—could stop him. He got hold of a gun and rushed to the house across the road. No, it wasn't the woman he wanted to kill, it was her cat, now quietly sitting on a dresser of the dining-room, thoroughly unconcerned and satisfied. Through the open window he fired, once, twice, three times, breaking pictures and glasses, like a madman, until the woman's son rushed with a gun and fired at him.

A tragedy. Amongst tears and sobs grandfather—badly wounded in the chest—was carried home, almost dying.

The woman's son ran off, trying to hide in the fields. The wrecking of two homes. The upheaval of a whole village.

And the cat? He had quite forgotten about the little finch—just an ordinary bird—and he never realized that the old man had been shooting at him. At the first shot he had jumped from his seat and climbed on the roof where—a white spot on the black tiles—he was now sitting quietly to watch the stars. And the stars—you can be sure of it—never took any notice of what had happened or of the humble roofs of the village lost among the mountains, though they kept glittering down so bright on them that one would have almost sworn they were only shining for those roofs, for them alone.

WHEN A BEAR WENT TO CHURCH

You may laugh or even frown—if you prefer it —at the idea that my story should deal with a bear who went to church.

In fact, although I am called an atheist and a writer of crazy fiction, I would have never dreamt of sending a bear to church unless this had really happened a few days before two young missionaries left for China.

A bear, as everybody knows, would not go to church just like a human being, to pray or to look round. He would go in as the result of some real and true miracle which is exactly what happened to my bear and two young priests. Of course, to believe my story one must have the same amount of faith as those two missionaries had, or else one cannot help laughing at the idea of the clumsy animal going to church because God had entrusted him with the task of testing the courage of two young priests on the eve of their departure for their mission.

However, here is our bear before the church, lifting with his paw the heavy leather curtain hanging across the door and getting inside. Then, a little at a loss, taking advantage of the semi-darkness of the temple and pushing himself through the double range of seats he bends low to look round and gracefully whispers to the nearest little woman kneeling in prayer:

"May I ask you the way to the sacristy."

Obviously the bear has a mission to fulfil and does not want to make mistakes, but the little old woman does not like to interrupt her prayers and without turning her head she points out with her finger to a corner of the church. Thus she does not know that a bear is near her or heaven knows how she would shriek.

The bear feels reassured. He walks straight to the spot and asks the sacristan: "Could you please tell me where is God?"

"God?" answers the sacristan, amazed.

"Yes, God. Doesn't He live here?"

The sacristan can hardly believe his own eyes.

"But you . . . you are a bear, aren't you?" he mutters.

"Yes, a bear, as you see. This is not a disguise."

"And how do you expect to have a talk with God?"

The bear looks at him with pitiful eyes.

"You should know that God converses with animals even better than with men. But now, tell me, do you know those two young priests who are leaving to-morrow for China?"

"Of course I do: one comes from Tuenno and the other from Flavion, three miles from here."

"And you must know that they have gone to their villages to say good-bye to their people and are expected back here to-night."

"Of course I do."

"You realize then that God has Himself given me all this information. Now I want you to know that God has also asked me and my little son to put these two young missionaries to a test and I must make no mistakes. That's why I am asking you for more details about them so as not to frighten undeservedly other innocent priests."

.   .   .   .   .

The scene here is represented with a certain malice which I am certain the two priests never intended when they first imagined it. That God should speak to animals easier than to men I

don't think anyone could doubt, especially when **one** considers that animals are always following nature (through which God speaks to them) while men (always doubtful and restless) are seldom conscious of their own actions and often even ignore those direct and definite ties which link them with God.

The fact remains that towards sunset, as the two priests were coming back to the Convent, just as they were leaving the mountain path to get on the main road, they found the way blocked by a bear and his cub.

It was springtime, when hungry bears and wolves no longer come down from the mountains in search for food, and at the unexpected sight of the two animals the young priests stopped with fright. They were unarmed, as priests should be, only one of them carrying a totally harmless stick picked up in the woods.

Almost instinctively they turned round, looking for help, but nobody was there who could help them except three pigs and little girl whom they had met when coming down the path. She was smiling at them as if unable to realize their danger and to see the two bears. How could she not be frightened by those two horrid beasts, so visible

264

across the road? Or did she think they were two trained and perfectly harmless animals? How could she keep on smiling merrily while the big bear was standing on his hind legs guarding the road, and the smaller one, ambling slowly forward on his short legs, was walking round one of the priests sniffing at him from all sides?

The poor fellow had instinctively raised his arms (perhaps to save his hands) and, not knowing what else to do, just watched the cub around him with his heart in his mouth. Then, unable to stand it any longer, he glanced towards his comrade and seeing himself in him as in a mirror, pale and haggard, all of a sudden, for no reason, flushed and smiled at him.

It was then that the miracle happened.

His friend, also for no reason, smiled back at him and the two bears, without anyone knowing why, suddenly turned their backs to the priests and went off towards the bottom of the valley.

They had made their test and their task was accomplished.

Unable to understand what had happened, the two priests watched for a long while the two animals in their sudden and unexpected retreat: then, amused at their natural awkwardness, they turned again to one another and unloaded their fears in a long loud laugh.

This, of course, they wouldn't have done if they had realized that these two bears had been sent by God to test their courage and that laughing at them was just as bad as to laugh at God. But they never thought of God, and they preferred to think that the Devil himself had put the two animals on their track. It was only later, when the bears, looking fierce and angry, turned round at their laugh, that they understood what had really happened. Had I been God I would have ordered those two animals to go back and punish the two ungrateful priests by eating them alive, but God, in His mercy, had already forgiven them.

By making the two priests smile at the sight of the bears God had shown that missionaries should know of no fear: by making them laugh at the retreating animals God had shown that the laughter was for the Devil, not for Him who had tested the courage of two of His servants.

No one, in fact, knows better than God, through His wide experience, that so many events which men, in their limited foresight, call evils are arranged by Him for their good, not by the Devil, as they often believe.

TORTOISES . . . FOR LUCK

Strange as it may seem, there are people in the United States who believe that tortoises bring luck, although even in the United States no tortoise has been found to be aware of its magic power.

Mr. Myshkow—for instance—has a friend who firmly believes in tortoises as soothsayers. His friend speculates on the Exchange and every morning—before giving his orders—he places a tortoise on the carpet of his drawing-room and watches: if the animal begins to move he is convinced that there will be a rally on the Exchange: if—on the other hand—the animal hides its head and refuses to move he is equally convinced that a slump is in sight.

Incredible: but more incredible is that he has always been right.

Having explained all this to Mr. Myshkow he takes him to his live stock dealer and makes him a present of a tortoise. "Keep it as a mascot," he says, "it will bring you luck."

With mixed feelings Mr. Myshkow rushes home, carrying the animal in his hand, afraid lest the stone—for it looks more like a stone in its cold stillness—would suddenly stretch on his palm its four clammy legs and poke out its wrinkled nun-like little head.

There isn't much excitement shown at home by his two children—Helen and John—at the first sight of the little animal which he carefully places on the drawing-room carpet.

Nothing indeed would arouse interest in those two prematurely aged children whose cold and dispassionate eyes contrast so strangely with the still young and lively eyes of their father.

Having stared for a few minutes at the little animal, John and Helen turn their slightly contemptuous gaze at their father who—stretched out on the carpet—is trying in vain to persuade the obstinate creature to break away from its stone-like pose and push its head out of the shell to admire its beautiful home. Then—suddenly and unceremoniously—John, impatient at his father's wheedling, puts out a foot and kicks the tortoise on its back. At once the little creature—attempting to recover its balance—puts out its four little limbs, its tail and the head, lashing the air painfully. Its pitiful struggle strikes a chord in Helen, who, feeling at last amused, bursts into a laugh, a shrill laugh like the shriek of a rusty pulley.

It is quite obvious that those children have no interest in the luck-bringing qualities attributed to the tortoise: to them the little creature on the floor is merely a rather dull toy which does nothing unless it is kicked about.

Mr. Myshkow is of course grieved: he hastily replaces the tortoise right-ends up and sadly watches it resume its stony trance. Almost unconsciously his eyes go from the tortoise on the carpet to the children and he is suddenly struck by the mysterious resemblance between those aged-looking human creatures, with their cold lifeless eyes and the stone-like tortoise. In fact, he gets alarmed by his incurable youthfulness in a world so obviously nearing decrepitude, almost feeling out of place, a man so perpetually young, in an age when children are born centenarians like tortoises.

And with a sad little smile at his children he sits down to watch the animal, fully convinced that it would be perfectly useless to explain to them why he had brought the tortoise home and why he believed in its magic power.

.   .   .   .   .

Of course Mr. Myshkow's knowledge of life has always been meagre. Although he has been married for over nine years, he has never yet understood by what mysterious fate he has come to share his life with a woman of such an inscrutable nature as Mrs. Myshkow, his wife.

How he has succeeded in becoming her husband, in daring to conquer her step by step, trembling at every move in case he offended her, he could positively never explain. In fact —after nine years of marriage—she is still a mystery to him, so entirely wrapped up in her cold porcelain beauty, so completely detached from the outside world of passion and love, that he still wonders every day why she has agreed to marry a man so exuberant, so everlastingly youthful. Is it any wonder that those two children, reared in that china-like body of a lifeless doll—have come into the world prematurely aged, like two sugar coated almonds from some forgotten vase?

Yet during these nine years of his married life

he has lived in perpetual anxiety lest his wife—
the inscrutable Mrs. Myshkow—would find some
pretext to divorce him. His fear has started on
the first day of their marriage, for—owing to the
way by which he had succeeded in winning her—
he was far from sure that she fully knew and
appreciated what marriage meant. Fortunately,
however, she knew it, but events had since shown
that she ever regretted those few moments in
which he had claimed her as his wife. Yet a
first child—Helen—was born and, later, a second
child, John. Each time she had retired for
several months to a nursing home in the country,
each time returning with a baby in her arms
that looked the image of old age. Not once had
she allowed her husband to accompany her or
even to visit her, so that—almost ignoring why
she had been away—he had found those two
children in the house like two little dogs pur-
chased during a holiday trip, unable even to find
out whether she is the mother and he their father.

.   .   .   .   .

Yet what surprises him most on that day is
that, while he is still kneeling on the carpet re-
storing the tortoise to its natural position, his

wife comes into the room and, seeing him bent on the animal rushes outside, goes to the hotel where her mother is staying and sends him a messenger with a written ultimatum: either the tortoise is to be immediately thrown out of the house or she will leave for London at once with her mother.

Mr. Myshkow is staggered: it has come at last, the futile pretext for a divorce. Well, he thinks, he is not going to give her the slightest chance. He immediately scribbles a polite note assuring his wife that she can safely come back and he will get rid of the offending tortoise at once. After all, he thinks, what made him bring home the tortoise? What greater luck could he ask for? Let the tortoise go back from where it came.

He picks the animal from the floor and holding it in his hand he tries to reach the shop where it was bought. It is getting late in the evening. Will the shop still be open? He will try. But where was the shop now? Oh yes, of course: on 49th street. This is the place, but the shutters are already down. Too late.

What can he do with the tortoise? Leave it outside the door all night? A passing taxi gives him an idea. He hails it, gives his home address and gets in. He will abandon the tortoise in the taxi and let it drive all night round New York, to pick up its luck.

But Mr. Myshkow has too warm a heart for animals: he would never allow an innocent tortoise to perish in loneliness. He must find a better place where to part with it. The taxi is now passing along Park Avenue with its chain of flower-beds down the middle. Mr. Myshkow has another idea. He dismisses the taxi and still holding the tortoise in his hand gently places the little creature on the ground among the flowers.

No sooner has he done this than a policeman looms over him from 50th street. He wants to know what he had been hiding amongst the flowers. A bomb, perhaps? No, it isn't a bomb, explains Mr. Myshkow with a reassuring smile which leaves no doubt as to him being incapable of hiding bombs amongst the flower-beds of New York. Merely a tortoise, a tame little animal. "No animals allowed here," thunders the policeman. Mr. Myshkow tries to explain: "It isn't exactly an animal: something between an animal and a stone: it hardly ever moves. Besides, urgent family reasons compel me to get rid of it.

It is supposed to bring good luck. Would the policeman accept it as a mascot? I'll make you a present of it."

"No," thunders the policeman, catching hold of his shoulder and pushing the man along the pavement.

What should Mr. Myshkow do? Still holding the unwanted animal in the palm of his hand, he decides to put it on the pavement whenever he is out of the sight of the policeman, but suddenly a better idea flashes through his mind.

After all, he thinks, the tortoise can have merely been a pretext for his wife to start a quarrel; if he gets rid of it to-night she will find another excuse to-morrow, one less likely to bring upon her the ridicule of the court. It would be silly to let the opportunity go.

Still holding the animal in his hand he begins to walk briskly home. His wife has returned. . . . She is sitting in the drawing-room reading. Without a word he kneels down and places the tortoise defiantly in the centre of the carpet.

The effect is immediate: the wife rises, rushes out of the room and returns in a moment, wearing her hat and coat.

"I'll tell the judge that you prefer the company

of a tortoise to my own," she says, and with a bang of the door she goes out.

Almost as if the words and the noise of the door slamming had found an echo in the tortoise's soul, its four little limbs and the tail emerge from the shell while a somewhat smiling little head peers out and the animal—now fully awake —sets out crawling round the room with an easy, happy, gentle swell of its heavy shell as no tortoise had ever done before.

Mr. Myshkow cannot restrain his surprise: the tortoise is telling him something. He remembers his friend's words. "When the tortoise moves it means things are going well."

"It's luck! It's luck!" he bursts out in the empty room.

MY LAST JOURNEY

Was it premonition or mere coincidence that made Signor
Luigi Pirandello write this as his last "short story" only a
few weeks before his death?
The title and theme, the pathos and feeling of hopelessness
expressed in this touching story cannot fail to impress those
who have followed Pirandello's work throughout his career.
They will find in *My Last Journey* a last and personal
farewell, only faintly disguised in his anonymous hero.

STARTLED from my sleep I find myself thrown out
of my compartment, in the middle of the night,
at a small railway station along the line.

I am alone and have no luggage.

I can hardly overcome my astonishment but
what seems most surprising is that I have not the
slightest bruise on me nor do I have the faintest
recollection of how all this happened.

I find myself alone, on the ground, in pitch
darkness, near a station where there isn't a soul
whom I can ask for guidance or help.

Worse still is the fact that I don't even yet
realize why I am making this journey: I have not
the slightest recollection of the town I came from

or the town I was going to when I fell here. I don't even know the reason for this journey nor whether I had any luggage with me when I started. I suppose I must have had none for I have none now.

The night is so dark that I cannot even see the name of the station, but I am quite sure that I have never been here before.

The large square outside the station is equally deserted. One solitary lamp is still burning at a corner. I get nearer the light, examining myself to feel if I am really alive. My hands go quickly over my body and I have no doubt that it is really myself walking in that strange deserted town at such an hour of the night.

Dawn will soon be here. Some time passes. I walk slowly towards the centre of the town as the sun rises and I see things which would astonish me were it not for a greater astonishment which seizes me in noticing that other persons like myself are now moving in the town, with complete ease and assurance, as if each of them knew what he was doing and was carrying on the natural course of life.

I am almost swept away by the crowd: yet something pulls me back, making me feel uneasy and

278

uncomfortable. I know nothing about myself, or who I am and where I want to go, while they seem so utterly sure of themselves and of their movements. Of course it is all my fault, not theirs, but however hard I try to do the same as they do something pulls me back again and makes me feel nervous and unsafe.

Can it be possible that I have reached my age without ever having done any work? Yet I know that I have worked hard, very hard. Was it only in a dream then? Why do other people seem to know of my work and turn round to look at me or even raise their hats when I pass by? Do they mistake me for somebody else? But nobody else is in front of me or at my back. Why then do they seem to know me and welcome me in this town where I don't recollect ever having been? Is it perhaps my dress? Am I dressed in somebody else's clothes? How could it have happened if I have no luggage with me?

Again my hands quickly feel my body and notice something hard bulging from an inside pocket. It is an old wallet, badly discoloured by time and by what looks like a prolonged stay in water. It cannot be mine: I don't remember having ever had such a wallet. With great care

I tear the two ends that have been matted together by the water. Amongst a few letters almost unreadable through the action of the water on the ink, I find a small sacred image, one of those which I used to receive every Sunday at church when a child. Stuck on its reverse side is a photo of the same size, the photo of a beautiful young girl, in a bathing costume, standing against the wind and stretching both arms towards me in a friendly greeting.

While I look at the beautiful girl I have almost the impression, if not the certainty, that that friendly smile and those two inviting arms are really pointing to me: yet, however hard I try to remember, I have not the slightest recollection of having seen her before. Could it be possible for such a lovely creature to be entirely wiped out from my memory, like a leaf in a storm? Why should I have placed her picture against the sacred image unless it were because she was the woman I intended to marry?

I carry on my search still further and from a hidden pocket of the wallet an old banknote sticks out, neatly folded and slightly damaged by the water. Judging by its discoloured appearance it must have slept there for years. It is a note for a large amount, now entirely withdrawn from circulation. I wonder whether it is really mine and whether I can use it as I have no other money on me. A restaurant is nearby and I begin to feel the need for some food. The manager, to my surprise, seems to recognize me and to treat me with extreme deference due to some exceptionally important client. Immediately a table is cleared for me, but I refuse to sit. I want first of all to discuss the note. The manager agrees that it is a very old one, but adds, for an important and well-known person like myself, the bank will be pleased to change it without any formality. He offers to accompany me to the bank where I am handed, in exchange, a large bundle of smaller notes, more than the small wallet could ever contain. I walk back to the restaurant but in the meantime the news that I am no longer a penniless man must have gone round, for on coming out I find a big car waiting for me with the driver, his cap in his hand, and holding open the door for me to step in. I don't know where he is going to take me but I begin to realize that as I have a car I must also have a home. Yes, I have a home, a beautiful old-fashioned place where my ancestors must have lived before me

and my successors will probably live after me.
But is all this heavy furniture my own? I don't
seem to remember the place. I feel a stranger in
it, almost an intruder. There is nobody I can ask.
It all looks bare and empty, just as bare and
empty as the whole town looked last night when
I was thrown out at the station. I try to make
myself comfortable but I feel cold and miserable.
I will not allow myself to give way and pacing up
and down the room I casually notice a door which
opens into a fully lit bedroom. On the bed the
same beautiful girl of the photo is reclining, her
bare arms outstretched towards me as an invita-
tion. I have no doubt. She is alive.

But where has she disappeared to?

Has all this been a dream?

At dawn, when I wake up from my sleep, she
has disappeared. The bed, so warm during the
night, has turned as icy as a grave. Where has
she gone? I am alone again. All round me is the
stale smell of a place where life is extinct, the
smell of old and forgotten furniture.

This cannot be my home. I am the victim of
a nightmare. No doubt I have been going through
one of the maddest dreams. Almost to reassure
myself I look at myself in a mirror hanging

on the opposite wall. Can it be true? Is that
aged face my own? Is that my real self? When
did I get so old? Who made me like that? How
did this happen so suddenly? Is this possible?
Or is it another dream?

There is a knock at the door. Somebody in-
forms me that my children have come to see me.

My children?

I am terrified at the thought of having any
children. When did I marry? When were they
born? Was it yesterday when I was still young?
If so, I shall be pleased to meet them now, at
once.

They enter the room, carrying in their arms
children of their own. They all come near me,
gently helping me to sit in an arm-chair and re-
proaching me for having got out of bed to
meet them. At your age, with such long trouble,
they say, you should be more careful. How do
they know? What do they know about my age?
How do they know that I can no longer stand on
my legs?

Sitting on the arm-chair I look at them,
listening to their warning almost as if I were the
victim of a gigantic joke.

But soon I realize that it is no joke. Is my life,

then, already at an end? Has this been my last journey? The farewell for ever before the Great Departure?

And while I watch them—their heads bent towards me almost as in prayer—I notice that suddenly lots of grey hairs seem to grow on them. It all happens under my eyes and I can hardly believe it. "You see," they seem to say, "this is no joke. Our own hair is turning white."

Even those of them who have stood by the door, little children still wobbling on their legs, have now come nearer and grown older while reaching my chair. One of them, a little child, has now become a promising girl whose arms are stretched around my neck, her head bowed on my chest.

I can bear it no longer. I feel that I want to stand and run away but I soon realize that no longer can I do what I like.

And through the same eyes, once so young and now so hopelessly aged, I stop to stare, motionless and dumb, at those kneeling near me, my white-haired children.

PUBLIC LIBRARY, RAWTENSTALL.